My Aunt Ruth

Also by Iris Rosofsky

MIRIAM

My Aunt Ruth
Iris Rosofsky

A Charlotte Zolotow Book

An Imprint of HarperCollins*Publishers*

Typography by Joyce Hopkins
1   2   3   4   5   6   7   8   9   10
First Edition

Library of Congress Cataloging-in-Publication Data
Rosofsky, Iris.
    My aunt Ruth / Iris Rosofsky.
        p.   cm.
    "A Charlotte Zolotow book."
    Summary: Sixteen-year-old Patty is pleased when her Aunt Ruth, a vibrant actress
who encourages her interest in the theater, comes to visit, but then serious complications in Aunt Ruth's diabetes threaten her ability to walk.
    ISBN 0-06-025087-9.—ISBN 0-06-025088-7 (lib. bdg.)
    [1. Aunts—Fiction.   2. Diabetes—Fiction.   3. Physically   handicapped—Fic-
tion.   4. Acting—Fiction.]   I. Title.
PZ7.R719565My   1991   90-4940
[Fic]—dc20   CIP
                                                                            AC

To Sharon, with love

My Aunt Ruth

1

I always knew when Aunt Ruth had come because of the sad, sweet scent of lilacs she left in her wake, sort of like the trail of foam a speedboat leaves behind— soft, ephemeral, dreamlike but not in a sleepy way— sparkling and full of life. Lilac Ambrosia was Aunt Ruth's favorite cologne. I also knew she had come by the odor of strong cigarette smoke that sometimes threatened to overwhelm the lilacs and by the occasional butt or powdery ash left in the ashtray or in a piece of aluminum foil she sometimes used for one. No one in our house smoked and Mother detested the habit and the befouling of the air. *"Nau*-zee-a-ting!" she pronounced. She kept one ashtray on the living-room end table to accommodate, reluctantly, the infrequent guest who simply must smoke. Aunt Ruth was the chief offender, although we only saw her once or twice a year. Mother was always quick to wash the ashtray and collect the little foil packets when Auntie left them around.

When I was much younger, I used to tiptoe into the

guest room where Auntie stayed when she was in town, closing the door quietly behind me. I'd open her wardrobe to sniff her blouses. Her blouses and her long silk scarves, most of which were purple, pink or fuchsia, smelled strongly of lilac. I liked to run them through my fingers and press my face into them; the soft, delicate fabrics became Aunt Ruth—they seemed to convey something of her essence.

Whenever Auntie came to visit, life at our house altered. There was an air of excitement and brightness, of something wonderful about to happen. I lived in anticipation of every moment I might spend with her. I insisted on sitting beside her at the dining table even though there were four sides to it and we each could have comfortably had our own side.

"Why don't you let Aunt Ruthie relax and have a little space for herself?" Mother prodded. "Sit at your own place."

"Oh, that's all right." Auntie laughed. "I have all the space I need. After all, how often do I get the chance to be so close to my one and only niece?"

Mother gave in, reluctantly.

Aunt Ruth was an actress and the most beautiful woman I had ever seen. Stately and slender, she had thick, wavy, copper-colored hair, which sparkled like shiny new pennies in the sunlight. When we were alone, she let me brush it and run my fingers through her waves. I was always eager to hear about her rehearsals and what it was like to be acting and walking around on a "set" rather than in a real room. Auntie most often acted in the daytime soaps. She never played a major role—usually a nurse in a hospital scene or occasionally the sweetheart of a doctor or a young lawyer. One time, when she phoned to let us know she was doing her best part yet, Mother let me stay home from school in the afternoon to watch her on TV. She played the girlfriend of a married doctor and there was one scene where she had a confrontation with his wife, who was crying and begging her to leave him alone. It was the first time, the only time, I glimpsed cruelty in Auntie. Afterwards, I was very upset. I could not reconcile what I'd seen with the sweet Aunt Ruth I knew.

"It's fantasy. It's only make-believe," Mother assured me, drawing me close so that my head rested on her bosom. "It's not meant for anyone to believe. They're only actors and actresses playing parts."

I knew that, yet it still upset me to see Aunt Ruth acting so mean. I was nine years old at the time.

Later, when I was in junior high school and Mother and Dad were both at work, I would play hooky whenever Auntie had a speaking role. Helen, my best friend from across the street, played hooky with me. We would come into the house through the back way to be less visible to the neighbors, and enter the kitchen. First thing, I would fix us peanut butter and jelly sandwiches and a plate of Oreo cookies while Helen poured two tall glasses of milk—so we wouldn't go hungry while watching Aunt Ruth. Then we settled down before the television. We usually remained to watch all the soaps until four o'clock, when the phone would ring. Mother called every day at four to make sure I got home from school safely and that everything was all right.

Mother worked as a stockbroker on Wall Street and Dad was a surgeon in a hospital in the Bronx. He was always gone by the time I got up in the morning. Both of their lives seemed to center around their work. Mother carried home a briefcase stuffed with papers, which she would work on at her desk in the den after supper. And Dad would spread out his mail and his insurance forms on the kitchen table and demand that I be quiet and leave the room as soon as I had cleared away my dirty dishes. So I would go to my room and telephone Helen, and when we had finished talking I'd open my books to do my homework.

Auntie's visits were always preceded by a telephone call a few nights before. Whenever Mother got off the phone with her, there were deep furrows between her brows and two long worry lines stretched across her forehead. They would remain until days after Aunt Ruth left.

"Don't let her upset you like that," Dad would say.

"I can't help it. She's my baby sister. I feel responsible."

"Well, you shouldn't. She's quite old enough to care for herself."

"I know, I know. But she's so *vul*-nerable. Things always seem to happen to her."

I wondered what "things" Mother was referring to.

2

It wasn't until I was sixteen and a junior in high school that I began to realize what Mother was talking about. Up until then, it had always seemed to me that Aunt Ruth must be the happiest, the luckiest woman in the world. She was beautiful, she was an actress, and she was married to a very handsome actor whom I occasionally saw on the soaps, but who never came east with her to visit. I had, in fact, only met Uncle Bob twice. (His real name was Robert but his Hollywood name was Cliff Daniels.) Once six months after they were married, when Auntie persuaded him to come to New York with her and meet his new family, and the other time when he had an audition here. But then he only stayed one night. He didn't talk much, and when he did, it was mostly about the important people he knew in Hollywood and how he hated New York because it was so filthy. When he didn't get a "callback" on the audition, he told us he was glad because he didn't think he could tolerate living "in the filth you call New York," where the series was to be shot.

Aunt Ruth's marriage had been a sudden event. We knew she was going with "a special someone," as she called him, but it wasn't until she phoned us one night to say they had just eloped that we realized it was anything serious.

"She has a way of jumping into things," Mother said. "I don't think it's good. She's too rash."

"Don't judge her so much," Dad responded. "She's old enough to know her own mind. How old is she, anyway?"

"She's thirty-six, but she seems like such a baby to me."

I thought eloping with her sweetheart was the most romantic thing a woman could do and I decided then that someday I would elope, too.

I was in my room one evening early in March, trying to work on a composition for English class, when the phone rang. Mom was visiting a client and Dad was at the hospital performing emergency surgery. It was Aunt Ruth. Her voice was very soft, almost muffled. She sounded as though she might be crying.

"How are you, darling?" she asked.

"I'm okay, Aunt Ruth. How are *you*?"

"Oh . . . I'll survive. As usual."

"Are you making any new movies?"

(She sometimes acted bit parts in movies, which I went to see two or three times.)

"No. Just the usual soaps." Then there was a slight pause. "Patty, baby. I can't stay on the phone too long. Is your mother there?"

"No. They're both out."

I sensed something was wrong. She always talked

a long time with me. "Is everything okay, Aunt Ruth?"

"Sure. Everything is . . . fine. I just thought I'd come for a visit. I wanted to know if it would be all right."

"It would be great! When are you coming?"

"How about tomorrow? I can make a nine A.M. flight so I should be at your house sometime late afternoon."

"I can hardly wait!"

"You're sure it will be all right with your mom and dad?"

"I'm sure."

"Good. I've got to run now. See you tomorrow, Patty."

"Okay. Good night, Aunt Ruth." And we hung up.

All the rest of the night I thought about Auntie and about how strange her voice had sounded. In bed I tried to imagine what the problem was. Did she miss out on a role she wanted? Did she have an argument with Uncle Bob?

At breakfast, when I told Mother about the phone call, she frowned. Then she murmured half under her breath, "I hope that husband of hers isn't giving her more trouble." I waited for Mother to elaborate but she didn't. That was the first inkling I had that Aunt Ruth and Uncle Bob were not getting along. I couldn't imagine how anyone could not get along with Auntie.

All during English and Social Studies that morning, my mind kept wandering. I'd never cared much for Uncle Bob; he only liked to talk about himself and he didn't hide the fact that he looked upon us as ordinary, nonartistic, dull human beings. He never looked you in the eye but was always gazing around the room when he talked. He didn't care about us enough to visit more than twice in five and a half years. I wondered what Auntie loved in him other than his good looks. Surely, she would not be fooled by surfaces.

Three days a week after school I had rehearsal for the Drama Club's production of *Our Town*. I was playing Rebecca, the kid sister of George, the romantic lead. I loved acting. Through it I was able to lead lives I never could have dreamed about—so much more interesting than waking up, going to school, coming home, doing homework and going to bed. And the excitement as opening night drew close was the most wonderful thing I'd ever experienced. It also made me feel closer to Aunt Ruth.

But this one time, I would rather have skipped rehearsal and come right home to be with Auntie. As it was, I didn't get home till nearly dinnertime. The house was dark and empty.

"Hello! Anyone home?" I called. But as soon as I stepped farther into the living room, I could detect the scent of lilacs and I knew Aunt Ruth had been here. I went upstairs to the guest room. Her valise stood unopened beside the bed. She'd brought more things than usual, as it was her regular, full-sized valise rather than her overnight bag. I hoped this meant a longer visit.

Dad came home at six and started fixing dinner. He was a better cook than Mother, and when he made supper it was always something special. Tonight it was baked macaroni with lots of cheese—a favorite of both mine and Auntie's. It was close to seven when Mother got home. She looked worn out and worried.

"Ruth won't be home for dinner," she announced.

"She phoned me at the office. She has a couple of urgent appointments this evening."

I was disappointed. I'd been looking forward to visiting with her in her room after dinner, to sitting on her bed and talking and watching her brush that magnificent copper-colored hair of hers. Sometimes she handed me the brush and sat down beside me. I always stroked her hair very gently for fear of hurting her.

"Come on!" she would laugh. "You can brush harder than that! I won't fall apart." When I'd brushed long enough, she'd say, "Now go bring me your brush and let me fix you up." I loved when she worked on my hair. And while she did, she would tell me bits and pieces about her life as an actress—things that were too minor to mention at the dinner table. They would only elicit a disinterested grunt from Dad and a noncommittal "Oh" from Mother. I knew she disapproved of Aunt Ruth's career—and was not thrilled with my interest in drama, either. But she never tried to discourage me. "I feel a youngster has her rights to choose her own interests," she would say, holding to it despite her obvious preference that I choose something else.

I loved the feeling of Auntie's fingers in my hair as she tried to arrange it in an upsweep or some sort of crown on top of my head. She always finished off by putting one of her own ornaments, usually a small fabric flower, into the back of the crown.

I waited up for Aunt Ruth in my own room that night. At about eleven o'clock I heard the taxi pull up in the driveway and the car door slam. When I heard

11

her tiptoe up the stairs, I opened my door. "Aunt Ruth," I whispered. Then I ran out into the hallway to hug her. Her cheeks were cool from the night air. She pressed me close and I could feel her stifled sobs.

"What's the matter?" I asked.

"Nothing, Baby. I'll tell you about it in the morning."

"Do you want to come into my room and talk?"

She smiled, and I noticed it cost her great effort. There were dark circles beneath her eyes. Her skin was pale, as though bleached by the moonlight, and across her forehead stretched two tense worry lines, which made her look remarkably like Mother. Her shoulders sagged with fatigue.

"Is everything all right?" I prodded. I didn't want her to realize I was alarmed by her appearance. But I wanted to know what the trouble was.

"Don't worry, Patty. Everything will be fine. We'll talk over breakfast. Wake me in case I'm still sleeping."

As she turned and walked across the hallway to her room, I thought I noticed her limping. I felt very uneasy as I returned to my room.

3

Auntie's door was still closed in the morning when I
left my room. I paused for a moment to listen for some
hint that she was awake. But it was silent. I didn't
have the heart to wake her, knowing how exhausted
she had been the night before. So I continued on my
way downstairs to the kitchen.

Mother was finishing her coffee. She looked deep in
thought, but glanced up when I came into the room.

"Is your aunt up yet?" she asked.

"No. I don't think so."

"I'll have to wake her in a little while. She has an
appointment this morning."

I decided to ask Mother what was wrong, though I
doubted she'd tell me.

"Your aunt is having some trouble with one of her
toes," she responded. "She's in a great deal of pain."

"Is that why she came to New York?"

"That's the main reason. She spoke with your father
on the phone and he recommended she see the chief

vascular surgeon at Montefiore. He set up the appointment for her."

I felt hurt that everyone had kept this a secret from me, though I knew there was nothing I could do to help. But I also felt relieved to learn that Auntie's problem was no bigger than a toe.

"Is that where she was last night—at the doctor's?"

"No. That was something else. She's going to see him this morning."

I wished Mother would let me accompany her; I tried to think of a way to convince her.

"You belong in school," Mother responded. "Aunt Ruth's visit is not a general holiday. I'm taking off from work to drive her and I'll wait with her and bring her home, so there's no need for you to come along."

That settled it. Whenever Mother used her "determined" voice and had that turned-down expression at the corners of her mouth there was no use arguing. So I gathered my books and set off for school. But I couldn't concentrate in any of my classes. I kept thinking about Aunt Ruth and wondering what was happening. During study period, I went to the phones in the main lobby and called home; but the phone rang and rang and no one answered.

There was no rehearsal that afternoon. I canceled a date I had made with Helen to help her select some proofs at the photographer's. I was anxious to get home.

Aunt Ruth was sitting at the kitchen table, her hands wrapped around a tall glass of tea with milk. She was the only one I knew who liked to drink hot tea from a glass. She said that was the way her grandma—my great-grandmother—used to drink it.

"The doctor said I need to be hospitalized," she told me, scarcely glancing up as I entered the room. "I'm waiting for the hospital to phone to let me know when they've got a bed available." I think she didn't want me to see how scared she was.

I fixed myself a mug of coffee and brought a plate of Oreo cookies to the table and set it down between us. I wasn't thinking as I shoved the plate towards her. I knew Auntie wasn't supposed to eat them. She was diabetic.

"No, thanks." She tried to smile.

"Can I fix you something else? A toasted bagel with cream cheese or an English muffin?"

"Thank you, darling. No, I'm really not hungry."

I sat down opposite her and commiserated in silence. I was trying to imagine how so small a thing as a toe could cause so much misery.

"How did you hurt yourself?" I asked. "Did you bang it or did someone step on your foot?"

"No. Nothing like that. It just happened, that's all. My toe's been hurting for months but I didn't think anything of it. Then, about two weeks ago, it started turning blue. So I called your father and he said to come to New York and have it looked at. It could be serious because of the diabetes."

Then we were both silent. I wanted to reach for her hand and hold it in mine as we sometimes did and as Helen and I occasionally did when there was a need for comforting. But Auntie's hands were still wrapped around the glass.

The phone rang. Auntie came to with a start.

15

"I'll get it! Sit there." I jumped up and ran for the phone. It was hospital Admissions. "Tell her to be here between four and six o'clock this afternoon," the voice directed.

"I'm all packed," Auntie said. "My little overnight bag is by my bed." She pushed herself away from the table and tried to stand, but her face pinched up in pain and she fell back into the chair.

"I'll get your bag, Auntie."

"I have to call a taxi."

"I can do that, too. You just sit." I had made up my mind I was going with her. I'd leave a note for Mother on the table.

"Does Uncle Bob know how serious it is?" I asked, when we were in the car and on our way.

"He knows it might be."

"Do you want me to call him and let him know you're in the hospital?"

She sighed. "No. Don't bother. He's got a lot on his mind without this." Then she forced a smile and said, "Let's talk about something more pleasant. Tell me about school and your rehearsals. How are they going?"

"She wants us off book by next week. I already know my lines. It's not such a big part. But I'm eager to start playing it, you know, not just holding the book and reading."

"I know. It's a lot better when you can look at the people you're talking to. Eye contact is very important. It's that way in TV, too, only it's not as natural as you've always got the camera right in front of you.

I'd like to try the stage someday. I think I'd like it."

She winced. I could tell the conversation was costing her great effort. When we were nearing the hospital, she spoke again. "I'd like to come see you in your play."

"It isn't for another month. You'll be in California by then."

"Maybe." She shrugged. "We'll see."

After a while, she added, "Maybe I'll try to get some acting in New York. As soon as my foot feels better."

We stopped at the main entrance and I helped Aunt Ruth get out. She was doubled up with pain. It was the first time I'd seen her slumped. I wanted to run into the lobby and get her a wheelchair, but I was afraid to leave her standing alone on the sidewalk. She looked as though she might keel over at any moment.

"Can you make it inside?" I asked.

"I'll try."

She grasped me under the arm. I felt pulled down by the weight of her body, apparently made heavier by pain and by the anxiety with which she hung on me. In my other hand, I carried her overnight bag, trying not to lose my balance as we walked.

Admissions only took a few minutes. I sat beside Auntie as she answered questions: her name, address, date of birth and health insurance coverage. She was not embarrassed about saying her date of birth in front of me. Now I knew for certain that Mother must be forty-nine, for she once let it slip that she was thirteen years older than Ruth. Mother was always so secretive about her age, you'd think it was some-

17

thing to be ashamed of. I couldn't understand it. I was sixteen and didn't care who knew it.

After Admissions, I wheeled Auntie to the blood lab, where they made her exchange the clothes she was wearing for a drab gray X-ray gown. They gave her a giant plastic bag, like a garbage bag, for her possessions. Then we went to X ray and sat a long time in the narrow corridor until she was called. And at last, someone escorted us upstairs to her room. By this time, Auntie was ashen with fatigue.

Her room, on the third floor, looked down upon the main entrance and the busy thoroughfare of doctors and nurses and visitors coming and going. It was an interesting point of view, but Aunt Ruth would not be able to see it from her bed. She was ordered to get into bed and stay there. I don't think she objected. It was a private room and the bed stood out in the middle. There were two chairs, a rolling table for meals, a sink with mirror, an olive-green metal locker and a toilet. Auntie didn't seem interested in any of it. She sat on the edge of the bed and removed her shoes, letting them drop to the floor. She closed her eyes and sat silently for a long time. I wondered what she was thinking. After a while, she sighed. "I could really use a cigarette." It was only then that I realized I hadn't seen her smoke at all since she came to New York.

"Have you quit?"

"I had to. A blue toe is an indication of poor circulation. Smoking constricts the small blood vessels."

"When did you stop?"

"About two weeks ago. Two weeks, one day and thirteen hours, to be exact."

"Do you miss it?"

"Oh, yes. Terribly. But I'm very scared. I made up my mind I simply must not return to it under any circumstances. So that's that."

I admired her determination. I unpacked her bag, setting her toothbrush, toothpaste and soap dish on the ledge over the sink, her nightgown and robe at the foot of the bed; I hung the clothes she had worn to the hospital on wire hangers in the locker, and put her magazine, book and transistor radio on the end table by her bed. They had given her paper slippers, so I left those on the floor and put her own shoes in the locker.

"I guess you won't be needing these for a while," I commented.

"I guess not. But I hate those paper slippers. I should have brought my own but I didn't think of it. Oh, well, it's only for a few days." She forced a smile.

Then we ran out of conversation. I sat in the chair by the bed and leaned forward to take her hand in mine. Her skin was soft and cool. I recalled that she'd once done a commercial for skin lotion. I bet Uncle Bob enjoyed holding her hand. I rubbed the back of her wrist softly with my fingers. At first, she seemed not to notice. Then she looked at me and smiled.

"Thanks, Baby. That feels good."

After a while, a nurse peeked in. "You just get yourself settled now, Ms. David. The doctor will be with you shortly." Ruth used her maiden name, which was Mother's maiden name, too. "My stage name has nothing to do with reality," she said. "It's nothing to do with who I am."

19

"May I have a painkiller, please?" she called after the nurse.

"Sorry. The doctor has to write orders for that. He'll be with you soon."

"How are you doing?" Dad was standing in the doorway. "My daughter taking good care of you, Ruth?" He grinned.

"Yes. Very."

"Dr. Keith knows you're here. He'll be in to see you tomorrow. How's the foot feel?"

"It hurts!"

"Well, just keep off it. Stay in bed. Don't get out for anything. Let the nurses get you what you need. That's what they're here for. I think about ten days of complete bed rest will do you a world of good. But that's up to Dr. Keith to decide. That's his field of expertise."

"Mitch, do you think I could get a painkiller?"

"I don't want to prescribe for you. Let the resident do that. It's that bad, huh?"

"Yes."

I wished there was something I could do to take away her pain.

Dad turned to me. "Come on, Bubbsy. I just finished a long day. I want to get going. Aunt Ruth has a phone right by her bed. You can call her tomorrow. Ruth, I'll stop by to see you in the morning. Sleep well."

"Thanks, Mitch. Good night." She reached her arms towards me and I gave her a big hug.

4

Ms. Howard called a full-cast rehearsal the following afternoon. I looked forward to rehearsals. I was beginning to love acting more and more. Performing before an audience was the most exciting thing I could think of. That moment just before the curtain rose, when a sudden hush fell over the audience—and that final curtain call, standing onstage with everyone applauding—those were truly magic times. I hoped to do my part well enough to be worthy of the applause. But as we got further into rehearsals, I found more than the anticipation of applause to stir me on. It was thrilling to be able to experience life—the life created by the dramatist—as the character, a person different from myself, would experience it. Of course, I was still myself. But I was also the character. And the set became my real world, at least for the duration of the rehearsals and the performances. I could put aside my own world and live the life of someone else in another time, another place. I especially enjoyed the roles where my character experienced deep emotions, for I could put myself into the character's skin and feel everything she was going through in my own soul.

So when Ms. Howard announced that Roberta, the girl who played the lead, had to drop out because of appendicitis and that she was holding auditions now for the role of Emily, I was excited. I wasn't happy about Roberta, but about the chance to try out for her role. In act 1, Emily, a high school student, is courted by George. In act 2, they marry. And act 3 has a very moving scene in which Emily, who has died in childbirth, comes back to earth for one more day. That was my favorite part of the whole play. I wanted to play Emily more than anything. I pictured myself trying out and getting the role and running to tell Aunt Ruth. How proud of me she would be!

Ms. Howard had made an announcement over the P.A. system in the morning that students interested in trying out for the role were to be in the auditorium at three o'clock.

I was surprised when Helen came marching down the aisle. She plopped into the seat beside me.

"Since when do you like acting?" I asked.

"Since you started telling me how wonderful rehearsals are. It sounded like fun so I thought I'd give it a shot. I don't expect to get anything, but it never hurts to try."

"Will everyone in the audience please keep still so the people onstage can be heard?" Then Ms. Howard called the first auditionee to read a scene opposite Larry, the senior who played George.

"Thank you very much," she said when they had finished. "I'll make my decision after I've heard every-

22

one this afternoon. You can either wait around or else I'll call you in the evening at home if you're the one. If you're leaving, though, please do so quietly. Next?"

I was relieved because Ms. Howard didn't seem particularly impressed with her. Neither was I. That was one down, about thirty to go.

The second auditionee was little better. She read the same scene—the one in which Emily and George first realize they're in love. Two down. Twenty-nine to go. I knew I could do much better. After a while, it became hard to concentrate on everyone's performance because I was hypnotized by hearing the same lines over and over. And because I was becoming increasingly nervous about my own audition.

Ms. Howard finally varied the scene. I was beginning to wonder how Larry could bear going over and over the same lines with each girl. Now she was asking the prospective Emilys to do my favorite scene, the one at the end where she comes back to earth. I hoped she would call on me. My fingers were icy and I was beginning to tremble. I knew I had a good chance because none of the girls so far had been very good. And I felt the part. I always cried when I read the scene to myself.

Ms. Howard read another ten girls in this scene before she switched back to the first. I was really beginning to get nervous now because three of the girls gave very good readings. I still thought I could do better, but I wasn't sure. I'd been hoping Ms. Howard would let me read the back-to-earth scene, but she called me for the drugstore scene. It didn't come out the way I would have liked. I felt I was standing out-

23

side the character, listening to every inflection. It didn't feel natural. Nevertheless, when I finished, Ms. Howard did say, "Very good, Patty," which she only said to the three other girls I also thought were good. So I stood a chance.

Two readings later, Ms. Howard switched back to the scene I liked. Why couldn't she have let me do that one? I realized I could have requested it and she probably would have let me. But it was too late now. She called on Helen. I wished her "good luck" and watched as she walked down the aisle and onto the stage. I wasn't worried about competing with her. She had never acted before nor shown much interest in it. But I was in for a surprise. Helen was extremely good. She acted with a great deal of feeling and even brought tears to my eyes despite my attempt not to be moved. As she read, I had a sinking feeling. I felt my chances slipping away. When she finished, a few of the students spontaneously applauded and Ms. Howard beamed and said, "Thank you very much, Helen. That was very fine, indeed!" I felt like crying. I told myself I mustn't be jealous, but I couldn't help how I felt. I wanted that part so badly.

As Helen approached me, she smiled nervously. I thought she looked triumphant.

"How was I?" she whispered.

She knew very well how good she was. She just wanted to hear me say it. But I didn't want to give her the satisfaction. I nodded and smiled and motioned to her not to talk while people were still auditioning. As she climbed over my legs and into her

24

seat, she took my hand and squeezed it. But I could not get myself to return the endearment.

There was little suspense after the audition when Ms. Howard stood up to announce the winner. Everyone knew it was Helen. I smiled and applauded with all the others and I told her I was "happy for her," but I really wasn't.

We had a "read-through" of the entire play that afternoon. I couldn't concentrate on my part. I was too busy thinking about the role I wanted and about how proud I would have been to tell Aunt Ruth that I had the lead.

It was after six when rehearsal ended. Ms. Howard said she wouldn't need me there Wednesday. "I'm just going to work with Emily, George and Mrs. Webb," she said. "I want to give Helen a chance to catch up with the rest of the cast, though I don't think she'll have any trouble."

I was secretly hoping that being unused to learning lines, she wouldn't be able to and that Ms. Howard would eventually take the part away from her and give it to me. But I didn't really think that would happen.

We usually walked home from school together whenever we could. But that afternoon I felt like being alone. I ducked into the girls' room, hoping Helen would leave without me. But she waited. I could hear her through the door talking with some of the other girls and they were all congratulating her and saying how wonderful she was. After a while, it grew quiet and I assumed Helen had left with the others, so I came out. She was leaning against the wall, reading her script and waiting for me.

"Are you all right?" she asked as I approached.

"Of course, I'm all right! Why do you ask?"

"You were in there such a long time I thought maybe you didn't feel well."

I thought she was just putting on her concern, to show that she was not only a good actress, but a good friend as well. So I didn't say anything more, but started heading for the door. Helen picked up her books, which were on the floor at her feet, and followed. The whole way home, Helen ran on and on about how happy she was to get the part. I felt like saying, "What are you making such a big fuss about? It's only a play. Imagine—a play where dead people talk and move around!" Only I didn't feel that way. The scene where Emily comes back to earth was the most beautiful thing I'd ever read. It always made me cry. And I loved the small-town New England life that *Our Town* depicted. I was still a part of that in my role of Rebecca, but it wasn't the same thing as if I'd been able to play the lead. So I listened to Helen in silence.

When we were most of the way home, nearly up to the point where we parted and went our separate ways, Helen noticed my silence, for she finally shut up. I felt a wall slip in between us. But I had no desire to breach it.

"'Bye," she said as she turned off on Oakdale Drive.

"'Bye," I responded indifferently.

5

When I got home, I wanted to go to my room, close the door and sleep, but dinner was already on the table. I wasn't hungry but I knew I'd have to eat if I didn't want a whole lot of questions.

"You're late," Mother remarked as I sat down. "Is everything all right?"

"Of course it is!" I was sick and tired of people asking me that. "Rehearsal lasted a long time." I didn't feel like mentioning the audition.

"Next time, if you know you're going to be late, please phone. We were worried."

"There's nothing to worry about. I can't walk out in the middle of rehearsal to call my mother. Do you expect Dad to walk out in the middle of operating to call you?"

Mother looked annoyed. "It's not quite the same thing," she said, getting up to serve me. "You want soup?"

"All right. But that's all I want. I'm not hungry."

"I saw your Aunt Ruth this morning," Dad said. "She said to give you her love."

"How is she?" Aunt Ruth was the only one I'd tell about the audition. She would understand.

"Her spirits were good. She was waiting to be taken down for a test."

"I'll call her after supper," I said.

"Don't do that. Not tonight. She went for an angiogram this morning. That's a very difficult test. She's probably all knocked out. I imagine she'll go to sleep very early."

"I'll visit her tomorrow after school."

"And when do you plan on doing your homework?" Mother asked. "You're spending so much time at rehearsals. You need to study, too, you know."

"I'll study when I come home."

"I don't want you staying up till all hours of the night."

"You treat me like such a baby. 'Call home, go to sleep early.' Next thing, you'll be giving me a bottle of milk to drink with lunch!"

"Don't be sarcastic with your mother," Dad said. "She only wants what's good for you. We both do."

"Well, it's good for me to see Aunt Ruth."

"And how will you get there?" Mother asked.

We had two cars, but they each used one for work. The hospital was in the Bronx and we lived in Westchester and there was no public transportation running in between.

"I guess I'll take a taxi." I had some money saved from working as a junior counselor in a day camp during the summer and from the babysitting I did during the year, though I was hoping to save much of it for college.

"You're going to use up your money pretty fast taking taxis," Dad remarked.

"I know. But I want to see Aunt Ruth."

"Why don't you wait till Thursday evening when I'm driving over to visit her?" Mother suggested.

It was because I didn't want to visit with Mother. I wanted to see Aunt Ruth alone—to talk to her in private. I couldn't be personal with her while Mother was sitting right there. Besides, I didn't like leaving Auntie alone in her room all this time.

Mother and Dad resumed their conversation while I ate my soup. They were discussing Aunt Ruth's condition.

"She'll probably have to lose that toe," Dad said. "It's gangrenous."

I tried to picture Aunt Ruthie with only four toes on her left foot. I wondered if she'd be able to walk. How awful to lose a part of your body!

Then Mother responded, "I'm sorry for my sister but in a way I'm not. She brought this all on herself."

"We don't know that. Medical science can't prove that. Some diabetics just seem to get all the complications, whether they've been controlled or not."

"My sister never took care of herself. She was always off her diet. Ever since she got diabetes—and I know it was a difficult age—she was only fifteen—but she always caused us such aggravation. My parents worried over her constantly. She had no will power at all. And the smoking—"

Dad sighed. "It's hard, Rachel. Believe me, I know.

29

Diets are the hardest thing in the world." Dad was overweight himself.

"Well, I do it," Mother said. "So she should be able to, too. Her life is at stake."

"I'm sure she does the best she can."

I felt close to Dad for sticking up for Aunt Ruth.

"Haven't you noticed," Dad continued, "that she's stopped smoking?"

"No! When?"

"The day she called me from California. She was plenty scared. I told her she'd better stop."

"You want something else?" Mother asked when I'd finished my soup. "You didn't eat enough."

"I'm not hungry."

"If you want something else later, there's roast beef and macaroni salad in the fridge. Meanwhile, why don't you go upstairs and start your homework?"

I had no intention of doing my homework. I was still depressed about the tryouts. I didn't feel like talking to anybody or doing anything. I just wanted to go to my room, get into bed, sleep and forget everything.

The next morning, Helen stopped by as usual on the way to school. "I want to go shopping this afternoon," she said as we walked. "I need a sweater and they're having sales now. You want to come with me? I'm taking the car."

"I'm visiting my Aunt Ruth. She's in the hospital. She may have to lose a toe."

"How awful!" Helen shuddered. "How are you getting there?"

"Taxi."

"You want me to drive you? I can drop you off and then do my shopping. And if you tell me when you'll be ready to go home, I'll pick you up."

It was hard to remain angry with Helen. I took her hand and squeezed it. She looked at me and grinned. "Okay?"

"Okay. Thanks."

When I passed the gift shop in the lobby, I remembered that Aunt Ruth needed slippers. I decided to use the money I'd saved on a cab to buy her a pair of blue furry ones that were in the window. Then I went upstairs.

Aunt Ruth was sitting up in. bed reading when I came in. She held her arms out to me and smiled. We hugged and then I sat in the chair beside the bed and gave her the gift.

"They're beautiful!" she exclaimed. "I'll enjoy wearing them as soon as they let me out of bed."

In the two days since I'd seen her, Auntie seemed to have grown paler. But perhaps it was just the drab hospital gown and the lack of makeup.

"How are you feeling?" I asked.

"Except for my toe, I'm fine. How are you doing?"

"Okay, I guess." And then I told her about the audition.

"Don't feel too bad," she said. "That's what show biz is all about. A dozen disappointments to every good role—if you're lucky."

"But I wanted that part so badly!" I could feel my throat tightening again at the thought of having missed out. "And besides, I wanted to know I was the

31

best." I finally added, "Of all people, Helen got it and she's never even acted before."

Auntie took my hand. "Don't be jealous, Baby. It'll only make you miserable and it won't change things. Just concentrate on putting all your efforts into your own role. Stanislavsky, the great Russian director, used to say, 'There are no small parts—only small actors.' You have to live your character's life to the fullest and she'll be just as important as any other character. Just as real—because you'll make her real."

"Do you think it means that Helen has more talent than I do? That she's a better actress?"

"You can't make those comparisons. She was better for the part. At least, in the director's opinion."

I wanted Auntie to assure me that I had more talent. But she didn't do that. I felt miserable. "Everyone applauded when Helen finished her audition," I said.

"So what?"

"They didn't applaud me."

"That doesn't mean anything."

"Yes, it does."

She was silent a moment. Then she said, "I'm sorry, Patty. I know how badly you must feel. I've been through it so many times myself. Believe me. I don't always get the parts I want. It does hurt. I know."

I thought about how proud I would have been to be able to tell Auntie I'd won the role. But now that pleasure wouldn't be mine. I thought of the satisfaction of being able to bring tears to people's eyes and to make them feel what I wanted them to feel. And how Helen would have the opportunity to do this while I wouldn't. My character elicited no particular emotions. She was cute and a little bratty and that was it. I thought of opening night and all the applause going for Helen. I hadn't had a good cry about it since the audition. Now, finally, in the presence of Aunt Ruth, I abandoned myself to my unhappiness. The sobs came heaving out of me. Auntie motioned me to sit beside her on the bed so she could hold me. I felt her arms gently close around me. And then my head was against her shoulder and I was crying uncontrollably.

"It's all right, I understand, it's all right, Patty," I heard her murmur. But my sobs drowned out whatever else she was saying.

I cried until I had cried myself out, and Auntie held me all the while.

It was growing late. Helen would be waiting for me double-parked outside the hospital, at five thirty. I had to leave.

"Tomorrow is rehearsal, but I'll come again Thursday with Mother. I love you, Aunt Ruth."

She smiled and gave me a quick hug. "I love you, too, Baby. Be well."

Helen was pulling up just as I stepped out the main entrance. I climbed into the front seat beside her.

"How's your aunt?"

"I don't know. I'm worried. She looked so pale." It was then that I realized I'd been so wrapped up in my own disappointments that I hadn't given Auntie a chance to tell me about herself.

"When is she getting out?"

33

"I don't know. Dad said something about ten days."

"Well, if you want to visit again, I can drop you off. Not this week because I have two reports due and I want to start working on my role and learning lines. But next week I can take you."

I wished she hadn't mentioned working on her role, but I decided that Helen was pretty nice after all and I wanted to remain her friend.

6

We worked on my main scene in rehearsal Wednesday. I knew all my lines, but even more than that I'd started inventing a life for my character beyond the play. I knew what her hobbies were and her favorite subjects in school. I knew what kind of friend she was and what she liked to eat for breakfast. I was beginning to feel her reality and I was able to get more into the role and to derive satisfaction from it.

Ms. Howard noticed the improvement, and I began feeling good about doing the part, even though it was a small one.

Thursday afternoon, Mother came home early from work so we could go to the hospital.

"Your Aunt Ruth may need surgery," she remarked as we were riding.

"Are they going to amputate her toe?"

"I don't think they're amputating anything, but it will probably be major surgery."

"When?"

"I don't know for sure. But soon."

I thought of Auntie on the operating table, unconscious, being cut open, but that picture made me very uneasy so I started talking about rehearsals. Mother's mind seemed a thousand miles away so I stopped talking and started thinking again. Close as Auntie and I were, she told Mother things she didn't tell me. I knew Mother spoke to her from the office once or twice a day. I had only visited her once and all I did was go on and on about myself.

Dad saw her every day, too. He was in contact with her doctors, so he would surely know what was going on. Maybe he told Mother. There was obviously a lot no one was telling me.

When we got to her room, a nurse was just leaving.

Auntie sighed and smiled to us. "They're in and out all day long. Trying my temperature, taking my blood pressure, bringing me medications, drawing my blood. A hospital is not the place to be if you need a rest."

Mother blew a kiss to Ruth. I leaned over to kiss her cheek but Mom pulled me back.

"Don't!" she warned. "Kissing spreads germs!"

"But I'm not sick. Neither is Auntie."

"You can't be sure. There's a lot of sick people in a hospital. The doctors and nurses and orderlies walk in and out of the rooms carrying bacteria around with them."

"They wash their hands." I thought Mother was being ridiculous. "Then how come you kiss Daddy?" I came back at her.

"I don't when he's in his scrub suit just out of the O.R."

"Well, what do you expect me to do—never kiss anyone?"

"Not in the hospital. A hospital is a filthy place." She wrinkled her nose to show her disgust.

I debated with myself for a minute whether or not to kiss Auntie anyway. But I didn't want to give her my germs if I had any. She had enough to deal with. I drew my lips tight to show my irritation with Mother. And I sank into the chair beside the bed.

"Do you know anything more?" Mother asked Ruth.

"Yes. They're operating tomorrow morning. I'm scheduled for seven forty-five. So I'll get it over with fast."

"What are they going to do?" I asked.

"It's bypass surgery. An artery near my foot is clogged. The blood can't get through. So they'll take a piece of vein from higher up and make a bypass for the blood. Dr. Keith has done hundreds of them and they've nearly all been successful."

"Then you'll be able to walk without pain?"

"As soon as I heal from the surgery."

"Mitch said he'd stop by in the morning to see you before they take you down."

Auntie smiled. "I'll probably be so doped up by then, I'll be out of it. They're going to sedate me while I'm still in the room."

"You've got an awful lot of courage," I said. "If it were me, I'd be a nervous wreck."

"I may not look it, but I am, and by morning, I'll probably be worse."

"But Dr. Keith is very good," Mother said. "Mitch says he's probably the best in the country."

"Yes, I know that. I have confidence in him. I'm just nervous about being cut up. And about being so helpless. I'll be completely in the hands of someone else. It's scary."

"Yes. I imagine it must be," Mother said.

And I thought, Especially for someone like Aunt Ruth. She's so used to handling her own life; making her own decisions.

We all fell silent for a while. I wanted to hold Auntie. But I was afraid of giving her germs before her surgery. I just sat there and didn't say anything. I noticed that the windowsills were lacking in greenery or flowers and I determined to bring Aunt Ruth a big bunch of lilacs next time.

Auntie appeared lost in thought. After a while, she sighed and said, "I never would have imagined a little pinky toe could cause so many problems."

Mother turned down the corners of her mouth. "You know you're a diabetic," she said. She sounded as though she were accusing her of something.

"I know, I know," Auntie replied. "But I still didn't think . . ." Her voice trailed off.

"Maybe if you had taken better care of yourself—"

"All right!"

Aunt Ruth's tone was sharp enough to keep Mother from proceeding any further along that line. But a moment later Mother added, "And smoking for all those years was about the most self-destructive thing you could have done."

"I know." Auntie sounded miserable. "But I did stop. Finally."

"After the cows escape, you lock the barn door."

"What do you want me to do? I can't turn back the clock and stop ten years ago!"

"What's the sense in talking about it?" Mother said. "I just feel terrible that you have to go through all this now. It probably could have been prevented."

"You're right," Aunt Ruth said. "There's no sense discussing it."

I felt that they'd been talking about something more than Auntie's smoking, something that went much deeper. It was obviously something that had been an issue between them for a long time.

I decided to change the subject. "Have you heard from Uncle Bob?" I asked.

"No. No, I haven't. He doesn't know I'm here."

"Haven't you called him?" Mother seemed dumbfounded.

"No." Then she added, "It would only upset him."

"I think he should know."

"No. Really. It's better this way," Auntie insisted.

But I was thinking, She must be lonely without her husband. Without even hearing his voice. She shouldn't be so concerned about his worrying. I decided to phone him myself when we got home.

As we were getting ready to leave, I wanted to say something to Auntie, to make her feel less alone. But I wanted to save my phone call to Uncle Bob as a surprise. He would phone her just before the operation, or just after and lift her spirits. For now, all I

39

said was, "I love you. I'll be thinking about you to-morrow." And I gave her a quick hug. Mother blew another kiss to her from the doorway.

As Mother was starting up the car, she sighed and shook her head. "I wish my sister weren't so irre-sponsible." But she didn't follow it up with anything.

After dinner, I went to my room to call Uncle Bob. I dialed the number directly and waited as it rang, planning how I would tell him about Aunt Ruth. One—two—three—then Uncle Bob's voice. "I'm sorry I can't come to the phone right now but if you will leave your name, phone number and a brief mes-sage at the sound of the beep—" I hung up. I hadn't counted on an answering machine. I'd have to try again later. Mother and Dad wouldn't be pleased with a whole lot of long distance calls to California. I phoned again at eight and still got the machine. I decided to try one more time. I forced myself to stay awake till nearly midnight to give Uncle Bob a chance to get home. I listened impatiently as it rang again. On the second ring, he picked up.

"Hello, Uncle Bob?"

"Yes?"

"This is Patty."

"Who?"

"Patty! Your niece."

"Oh, yes." After a brief pause, "How are you?"

"I'm fine. How are you?"

"Fine." (Another pause.) "What can I do for you?"

I hated when people asked that. It made me feel I

had called to beg a favor. "Nothing. I called to tell you something."

"It's about Ruth, of course. What is she, dead or something?"

I was taken aback by the anger and coldness in his voice.

"Of course not! But she's in the hospital. She's having surgery tomorrow."

"Why tell me? Does she expect me to jump on a plane and fly to her bedside? Any mess she's in, she did it to herself."

I couldn't understand. Everyone seemed angry at her for getting sick! First Mother, now Uncle Bob. It wasn't her fault.

Uncle Bob continued. "She smokes up a storm. There's no controlling her. I tried to get her to quit a dozen times. So did her doctor. But your Aunt Ruth is a very stubborn lady. So now she's paying the piper. And she expects me to set aside my own life to come and be with her? You can just tell her—"

"Wait a minute! Auntie didn't tell me to call you. She doesn't even know."

"Well, you can tell her anyway from me that I'm glad she's in the predicament she's in. Maybe it will teach her a lesson."

I wanted to tell him what a bastard he was, but I was afraid he might take it out on Auntie. I mumbled, "Sorry I bothered you." And I hung up.

I sat on the edge of my bed, stunned. It was awful, the way he spoke. He didn't care about Auntie at all. All he thought of was his "own life." I wondered if that was part of the reason Aunt Ruth seemed so worried and sad. Or was it all because of her foot? I was overwhelmed with sadness for Auntie. It must be terrible to live with someone who didn't care at all. I wondered if she still loved him. I felt she did; and that made it worse.

I decided not to mention the phone call to anyone. Maybe they'd had an argument and he'd get over his anger in a few days. Auntie would feel terrible if she knew what he'd said.

When I finally crept under the blanket and closed my eyes to sleep, I kept thinking about the two of them, trying to imagine how it was for Aunt Ruth to live with an angry, bitter man who cared only for himself. Or was it possible that she imagined he loved her. Could love be that blind? Auntie was so beautiful and sweet she could get any man she wanted. Why stick with Uncle Bob? It was difficult to understand. My thoughts ran in circles until finally I drifted off to sleep. The next thing I knew the alarm was ringing. I felt so weary I could scarcely lift my arms. I wanted to turn over and go back to sleep. But it was morning—time to start a new day.

7

As I was dressing and through breakfast, I kept running that phone conversation through my mind. I felt
I would burst if I didn't share it with someone, so I
decided to tell Helen.

As we were walking to school, I relayed the conversation to her.

"I don't know," she said after listening to me. "I
don't think that means he doesn't love her. My parents
argue all the time yet I'm sure they still love each
other."

"They may argue, but they don't say such terrible
things, do they?"

"Worse. Much worse."

"How come you never mentioned it?"

"I don't know. I guess I just assumed most parents
argue like that. Don't yours?"

"No!"

"Never?"

"Sometimes they argue, but never like that. They
may disagree about something or maybe Dad doesn't

like the way Mom did something. He's very fussy about having things done his own way. But he never wishes her dead or sick or anything like that."

"How do you know?"

"I know, that's all."

I was shocked at what Helen told me. I'd been in her house often and her parents seemed to get along fine. But maybe that was the show most married couples put on. Or perhaps Helen was making it up to make me feel better about Aunt Ruth and Uncle Bob.

I phoned the hospital three times between classes. It was hard for me to concentrate on anything but Aunt Ruth. It's funny, I never really thought of her as having problems. But now, suddenly she seemed beset with them. I had always thought her life in Hollywood was so glamorous and that she must surely be very happy. I was beginning to see how appearances can prove deceptive.

Each time I called the hospital, they said she hadn't come back to her room yet. I was very worried, so I phoned Mother at her office. She said she spoke to Dad and that the operation was turning out to be more complex than anyone had expected. That was three o'clock, just before rehearsal—and she was still on the operating table.

"Don't worry," Mother said. "She's in very good hands. She'll do fine."

I tried to concentrate on the play and to imagine myself inside the character, but I couldn't do it. I was glad when Ms. Howard decided to work on some scenes I wasn't in and she excused me.

Dad came home a few minutes after I did at five o'clock.

"Your aunt's doing very well. I looked in on her in the recovery room. She was still sleeping. It was quite an ordeal. Dr. Keith worked on her for over seven hours."

"Was the operation successful?"

"I certainly hope so. They had some problems there for a while. Dr. Keith's original strategy didn't work. It should have, but it didn't. So he had to devise something else. But that seemed to work fine. I don't think we have anything to worry about."

"When can I call her?"

"Not tonight. She'll be out of it. We'll all go over to see her tomorrow."

The next morning was Saturday. I was dressed and ready to leave with Dad when he made his rounds. Visiting hours didn't start officially until eleven o'clock, but Dad would be able to get Mother and me in with him.

Dad said to wait for him in the lobby while he went to see his patients.

"Let's go into the coffee shop," I suggested to Mother. I'd had breakfast and coffee at home but that was two hours ago and I craved more coffee. I drank it black and strong.

Mother made her disapproving face. "You drink entirely too much coffee."

"I only had one cup this morning."

"It was a mug—the large mug. All that coffee isn't good for you. That caffeine isn't good for anyone."

45

I wondered if Mother was health-conscious before she married Dad. The two of them washed their hands about a hundred times a day. Dad was always lecturing me about the dangers of hepatitis or some other contagious disease, which, he said, often came from not washing before eating. After a while, I started going to the girls' room to wash every day before lunch. Some of the girls teased me about it and one of my classmates started telling everybody that I thought I was better than they were. She called me Ms. Purity. It made me angry but I tried to ignore her.

Mother wouldn't join me so I went into the coffee shop by myself. The aroma of good strong coffee was everywhere. I sat on one of those round swivel stools at the counter and ordered a cup. I wrapped my hands around it and watched the steam rise up from the surface in fragile curlicues. The coffee shop was a busy place so early in the morning. To my right were three young doctors, stethoscopes dangling from their necks, wolfing down eggs and bacon and talking loudly amongst themselves. Mostly there were hospital employees around the counter; it was too early for visitors. Muffins and Danishes were neatly stacked in plastic-covered containers spaced at intervals along the counter. I ordered a corn muffin to eat with my coffee. The sight of everyone else eating made me want something, too. As I ate, my gaze fell on the glass doors leading to the lobby where doctors and nurses were coming and going. I thought of Aunt Ruth, confined to bed, eating her breakfast off a tray, removed from all this activity and life. I bet she felt terribly

46

cut off. Well, soon we'd be surrounding her bed, all talking at once and she'd be telling us when she'd be coming home. I must have been daydreaming a long time, for when I looked up, Dad was standing outside the door, motioning to me. I stuffed the remainder of the muffin in my mouth, took a big gulp of coffee, paid my bill and left.

"Come on, Kid. I got a busy day ahead. I can't stand around waiting for you," he said, putting his arm around my shoulder. "How many times do you have to eat breakfast, anyway? If I ate like you, I'd be as fat as a blimp."

We walked down a long narrow corridor to the elevators. "She's in Intensive Care," he said. "It's routine for anyone just out of bypass surgery."

As we neared the I.C.U., several nurses greeted Dad. "Good morning, Doctor." "Good morning, Doctor." He smiled and waved. "Good morning, good morning!" He turned to me just before we entered the room. "You're going to see some pretty sick people here. They've been through every imaginable kind of surgery and some pretty unimaginable kinds, too. Some have tubes coming out of them wherever a tube could be inserted. So don't be alarmed at what you see."

Dad entered first, then Mother, then I. Auntie was in the first bed near the door. She was lying back on her pillow, her eyes closed when we came in. Overhead, an intravenous bag was suspended from a pole, attached to her right arm via a long, thin plastic tube.

"Wake up! Wake up!" Dad called. She opened her eyes and smiled weakly.

"Hi. I wasn't really sleeping. They don't let you sleep around here. Someone was just in to take my vital signs."

"Why don't you eat your breakfast? It'll get cold."

"Where is it? I didn't see it. I'm starved." She started to sit up, then dropped back on the pillow. "I guess I'm a little weak." She tried to smile but it seemed a great effort.

"How do you feel, Aunt Ruth?"

"Oh, Patty, Baby. I'm all right. They say the operation went well. That's all I care about." She sighed. "If they'd just stop bothering me I could sleep for another twelve hours. I'm exhausted."

Mother nodded. "You do look tired."

"Tired isn't the word for it!"

"Does the doctor say when you'll be coming home?" I asked.

"I haven't seen him yet this morning. He stopped by while I was in the recovery room. He seemed pretty pleased. But he sure had to work hard. Seven and a half hours!"

She was pale and she looked as though she'd lost weight. Her lips were dry and white at the corners.

"Can I raise the head of the bed for you?" I asked. "Then you'll be able to eat."

"These beds don't go up."

"You want to sit?" Dad asked. "I'll help you."

I walked to the other side of the bed where her breakfast tray was on a rolling table. "Let me help you, Auntie."

"I'm okay, Baby. Thanks." She reached for her cof-

48

fee. "They don't allow you anything down here. Not a toothbrush or anything. I feel so grungy."

"Start eating and you'll forget about that," Dad said. "Where do you see room around here for personal belongings? You'll be going upstairs soon anyway."

"When?"

"I don't know. Maybe tomorrow. Or the next day."

"These eggs are cold. But I'm so hungry I don't even care."

I glanced around the room. The other three beds were occupied. Anonymous white mounds of blankets and sheets with a head poking out here and there. The patients seemed very old. I could see only two faces, both with their mouths open, toothless, gaping black holes. A machine by the bed next to Auntie's was breathing for the patient—Whirr—shhhhh! Whirr—shhhhh! Imagine—having to depend on a machine to breathe—and if something goes wrong or someone accidentally pulls the plug—! I shuddered.

Aunt Ruth smiled. "It's not too pleasant in here, is it?"

"You want me to get you a magazine or something?" I asked.

"That would be nice. Thanks."

Just then, a nurse came in. "Sorry. Only two visitors at a time. Someone will have to leave." She looked at me. I met her stare and didn't move.

"I'm her doctor," Dad said. "So I don't count."

The nurse looked suspicious, but she left.

A moment later, a team of young doctors entered and surrounded the bed.

"Doc! Fancy meeting you here. How are you?"

"Not too bad. Still kickin'. You taking good care of my sister-in-law here?"

"You bet! We just came to examine her."

"You want us to leave?" Mother asked.

"That's not necessary. We're only going to feel her pulses. May I?" he asked Aunt Ruth, with one hand on the blanket ready to pull it aside.

"Go ahead."

"You had a nice strong pulse there in the recovery room."

"We're just checking," one of the other interns added.

The doctor felt her ankle and then placed his second and third fingers on one spot and held still. We all waited silently. He kept his fingers in place a long while, an intent expression on his face. Then he tried another spot.

"What is it? Don't you feel the pulse?" Auntie's face had filled with fear.

"Shhh! I don't know. Wait a minute. It was there a few hours ago. It's got to be there. Here—you try," he said to one of his teammates. The other doctor pressed the same spot, then probed her foot and squeezed it elsewhere.

"Nothing," he said.

"Let me try it." Dad took over, pressing here and there on her ankle, finally settling on the original spot and holding his fingers there. Meanwhile, the fear in Auntie's eyes turned to panic, like an animal caught in a trap.

"Don't you feel it, Mitch?"

"No, I don't, Ruth."

Tears ran down her cheeks.

"Don't cry. We'll get Dr. Keith in here."

"I'll get him, Doc," one of the interns volunteered, running for the door.

"There may be nothing to worry about," Dad said. "Let's see what Dr. Keith says."

I touched Auntie's hand. It was icy-cold. I held it in mine and tried to warm it, wondering all the while what was going on.

Dr. Keith, a trim, serious man about Daddy's age, entered swiftly, trailed by the intern.

"Good morning, Mitch. Good morning." He nodded to Mother and me. "You're having some problems?" he asked Ruth.

"I guess I am. They can't find my pulse."

"I know, I know. Let's have a feel."

"I'm frightened."

"There's nothing to be scared of yet. I'll tell you when to be scared."

He leaned over and pressed her ankle and we all kept still. I could tell Auntie was holding her breath. Dr. Keith peered into space as though he were listening intently to very complex music. Then he relaxed his hand and straightened up.

"You lost your pulse, Kid," he said to Auntie. "I'm very sorry. I don't understand it. You were doing so well a few hours ago. I simply don't understand. That surgery should have worked. It should have held up."

"Is it time for me to be scared now?" Auntie asked, attempting a smile.

"No. Not yet. We're not giving up on you. We're

51

going to do it over. Stan," he said to one of the interns. "Book us into the first available O.R."

"You're going to operate again—today?"

"Yes ma'am. As soon as we can. We can't afford to waste time. You're a strong woman. You can handle it."

"And what if this one fails, too?"

"Think positive! If this one fails, we'll do another on Monday. I'm not giving up, I told you. If it's at all possible, we're going to save that leg."

"You mean—I might have to lose my leg?" Auntie grew white as the sheet she was covered with.

"I hope not."

We were all stunned. No one spoke after the doctor left. Then Auntie said, "I can't believe it! It's—like one of those hospital soaps I act in. Only this is real!"

8

I thought about Auntie all day. There was nothing I could do to help her. I phoned the hospital three times. At a quarter to four they said the O.R. had just called for her. I pictured them rolling her through the halls on a stretcher and then into the operating room. She would be lying on a cold hard table surrounded by strangers in green gowns and masks, only their eyes showing. I wished I could be there to hold her hand and to comfort her. If only Uncle Bob were waiting for her when it was finished. Maybe then it wouldn't be so bad for her. But, knowing how Uncle Bob didn't care, it was better that he wasn't there. I wondered if Auntie knew how selfish he was and how nasty. She'd lived with him five years; she must know, I thought. How awful for her when this is over and she returns to him. If, God forbid, they have to amputate, he probably won't even help her.

I was alone in the house, supposedly writing a book report due Monday. Mother and Dad were out shopping. I called Helen. I had to tell someone about Aunt

Ruth. Helen was a terrific listener. But she was at a special rehearsal with Ms. Howard. I felt I would burst if I had to stay in my room and work. So I took my pocketbook and set out to walk the mile and a half to the shopping mall in White Plains. Shopping for clothes always made me feel better. I wanted something frilly and feminine for Aunt Ruth; I finally settled on a satin bed jacket. The shopping didn't relax me, though I felt good about getting something for Auntie. Twice I hunted up a public phone to call the hospital; both times they said she was still in the O.R. I thought of her lying there with her leg cut open and Dr. Keith working desperately to get her blood to flow through the bypass. It was a mercy that Auntie could sleep through it all. I called Mother to tell her where I was so she wouldn't worry. For a change, she didn't ask me if I'd done my homework. All she said was, "I just got home. Daddy dropped me off. He went back to the hospital to see how things are going."

"She's still in the O.R.," I said.

"This type of operation is always a lengthy procedure. It's very delicate surgery."

And then I broke down crying. Right there at a public phone in the middle of B. Altman's.

Mother said, "Patty, honey, why don't you come home? You'll feel better."

"I'm all right."

"I'll feel better, too, Patty. It's awful here alone. I can't stop worrying. Take a taxi, honey. Please. I'll pay for it."

It was the first time I could recall that Mother said she needed me.

When I got home, Mother met me at the door and hugged me tight. I began crying again and she patted me softly on the back as though I were her little baby. Then she led me into the kitchen and asked if I was hungry. I hadn't eaten since the hospital. I was starved, only I hadn't thought about it all day. Mother heated up some soup for both of us.

"Daddy may be late," she said. "He wants to look in on Ruth in the recovery room. So there's no sense waiting for him."

At about nine o'clock, Dad called. I listened in on the extension.

"I'm on my way home," he said. He sounded exhausted.

"How did it go?" Mother asked.

"It failed. I'll tell you all about it when I get home. They're going to operate again Monday morning."

"Shall I fix supper for you?"

"Don't bother. I ate at the hospital. See you in about half an hour."

"How many times will they operate if it keeps failing?" I asked Mother.

"I'm not sure. I think Dr. Keith said three."

"Then what?"

"I don't know. But I'm sure everything will work out. Dr. Keith is a very fine surgeon." Then she added softly, "I can't picture my baby sister as an amputee. It's got to work."

But Dad didn't seem too confident when he came home. "They knew almost from the beginning this time that it wasn't going to work. They ran into trouble right away. Everything went wrong. She kept clotting. They couldn't get the blood to flow through the bypass."

"She won't lose her leg, will she?" I asked.

"I don't know. I hope not."

I was overwhelmed with fatigue. I'd been tired all day but I hadn't allowed myself to think about it. I could scarcely get upstairs to my room. I felt leaden. I got undressed and turned off the light, not even bothering to brush my teeth or to wash, and fell asleep as soon as I got under the covers.

Dad didn't leave for the hospital till ten o'clock the next morning. He never made rounds on Sunday. He was just going to see Aunt Ruth. Mother was going with him and I wanted to go, too.

"We're only going to stay a few minutes. I don't want to tire her out. She's already very weak and she has more major surgery tomorrow."

"Please!"

"Are you ready to go right now? I'm not waiting for you. I've got a lot of things to do today."

"I'm all ready."

It was a chilly, gray morning. I sat in the backseat staring out the window. The trees weren't budding yet. There were just bare branches. In a few weeks it would be different; spring would be here. If I wanted to bring Auntie flowers, I'd have to buy them. Our lilac bush was still asleep. Mother and Dad spoke softly in the front seat. But I didn't try to hear what they were saying. I was too tired.

We parked in the garage and walked across the

street to the main entrance. The security guard waved us through although we were too early for visiting hours.

"Morning, Doc."

"Good morning, Jason. How are you?"

"Can't complain, Doc."

Dad knew everyone and everyone knew Dad.

Aunt Ruth was sleeping when we came in but she woke up right away, as though sensing our presence. She attempted a smile, but her eyes were clearly not smiling.

"Hi. Thanks for coming."

"How are you feeling?" Dad asked.

"All right, I guess. Very tired. My leg aches. I wish I could change my position."

"Just don't move the leg."

"Could you get me something for pain? I asked the nurse twice already but she's too busy." Then she added, "I guess you know already. The operation failed. Dr. Keith was in to see me a couple of hours ago."

"I know. I spoke to him last night. I looked in on you in the recovery room but you were completely out."

"Mitch, what do you think is going to happen?"

"He's going to try again tomorrow. He's not giving up."

"And if that one fails?"

"We'll cross that bridge when we come to it."

She looked Dad in the eyes. "You don't think they'll have to amputate, do you?"

"I don't know," he said softly.

Just then the nurse came in and told us we had to leave. "She needs all the strength she can get. She needs to rest." I told Auntie I'd call her tomorrow.

"No, don't," she said. "It'll probably be another long operation. I'll be out of it afterwards."

"You can't call her," Dad said. "Where do you see a phone in here?"

I looked around. There was none.

"As long as she's in intensive care, you can't call her. Ruth, we gotta go. I'll look in on you when you're out of surgery. But you'll probably be sleeping."

I wanted to give her a hug and a kiss, but Dad said, "Better not. She doesn't need a cold now on top of everything else."

I didn't have a cold, but there was no sense arguing.

I didn't see Auntie again until Thursday. Mother took off early from work so we could visit before supper. Ruth was back in a private room sitting up in bed reading when we came in. I brought the bed jacket with me all nicely gift-wrapped in lavender and blue tissue paper with a big satiny bow. She smiled when she saw us and put down her book. She looked happy—still pale and worn, but happy.

"How are you feeling?" Mother asked.

"Great! Tired—but great. Relieved!"

"I bet!" I said. Dad had told us that things had gone well this time. "I'm so relieved it's over with," she continued. "I don't think I could have borne another operation. Dr. Keith says I should be able to be discharged in about two weeks."

"I can't wait!" I said. "You'll be staying with us, won't you?"

"That's up to your mom and dad."

"Of course, you will!" Mother said. "You know we'd love to have you. It may be difficult for you getting around in the beginning. This way you can take it easy. We can do for you."

"That sounds good. Thank you."

"You don't think it will upset Bob too much, do you? Your being gone so long. He's welcome to come and stay with us, too. I hope he knows that."

"He does. Only, he's all wrapped up in auditions. He told me before I left that I shouldn't expect him to come. He doesn't like me to make demands on him."

"That's hardly a demand. You've been through a lot. You need your husband. You need all the support you can get."

"I know. But that's all right. I'll manage."

I thought if I was married and in the hospital and my husband didn't come to see me, I'd divorce him. I couldn't understand why Aunt Ruth excused him. I thought of my phone conversation and wondered if she knew how nasty he was.

"Does he know about all this surgery?" Mother asked.

"No. He thinks I came to have my toe examined. He was really sore, too. He said there are plenty of good doctors in L.A. I didn't have to come to New York."

"He misses you."

59

"I doubt it. He thinks I'm wasting money." She was thoughtful a moment. "Maybe I'll call him tonight now that I've got a telephone."

Then she changed the subject. "How are rehearsals coming along?"

"We're off book in act one already. It's fun. I'm getting a real feel for my character."

"Good! Keep it up."

"I don't think she's finding enough time for her other schoolwork," Mother complained.

"Yes, I am!"

"I'm sure she's doing fine. I've got confidence in Patty." Aunt Ruth winked at me.

Mother shot her a dirty look. I feared the approach of the familiar argument. "Your academic work comes first," Mother would say. "After that, you can go in for dramatics or whatever else you want. Play-acting isn't going to get you into a good college."

Every time she linked drama with "whatever else," I got the feeling she was putting it down. To her, drama, volleyball or the sewing club were all the same. I couldn't make her realize that I was serious about acting. It was more than wanting to be like Aunt Ruth.

I'd rested my gift on the windowsill when we came in and then I'd forgotten about it. "I got you something," I said, handing her the box.

"Oooh! What is it? Thank you, darling. But you shouldn't be spending your money on me."

"I wanted to."

"Such pretty wrapping! It's a shame to destroy it."

"Go on, open it!"

"It's beautiful! A perfect match to the slippers you bought me!" She reached out to hug me. "It's all right," she assured Mother. "The germs won't hurt me. My surgery is finished."

"I don't want Patty getting germs either," Mother said.

"But I'm not sick."

"Maybe. But you come into contact with the nurses and doctors who have just been in contact with other patients who are sick. Most of them are very sick or they wouldn't be here."

"This is a surgical floor."

"Still and all, that's how diseases spread." Mother never let go.

We stayed about an hour. Auntie began to look tired, so we left. I couldn't come back for over a week because of midterm exams. And then Ms. Howard increased the rehearsal schedule. We were rehearsing on Saturdays now, as well as during the week.

But I talked to Auntie on the phone. A few days after our visit, she said, "You know, Patty, I called Bob and I was really glad. He was so sweet. When I left California we were both upset, but all that's cleared up now. He said he'd try to come to New York to be with me." I was glad for her. Maybe I'd been mistaken about Uncle Bob.

The next time we spoke, she had started physical therapy. "I'm able to stand—with help," she said. "I'm wearing those slippers you bought me. On my good foot anyway. Thank you. They're lovely." I told her about rehearsals and how much I missed her.

"I'm looking forward to seeing you in the play," she

61

said. "I should be discharged in about eight or ten days. They still have to remove my staples."

"Staples?"

"They're stronger than stitches. I've got a whole line of staples from my groin to the sole of my foot. I look like the original Zipper Lady. I hope nobody walks by with a magnet." She laughed.

It was good to hear her laugh.

"I've gotten through the first ten days safely. Dr. Keith says I'm 'home free.' We just have to wait for everything to heal."

The next time I visited Aunt Ruth she was walking in the corridor with a walker. I saw her, as soon as I got off the elevator, in her powder blue dressing gown, one of the slippers I bought her and sort of an open clodhopper on her "bad" foot. She was walking very slowly with great effort. When she looked up, I motioned for her to take her time. She gave me a big warm smile and continued her pace towards me. Her hair was pinned up on top of her head, but soft and wavy around her cheeks. She was wearing makeup and beginning to look like her old self.

"How are you, Cookie?" she greeted me.

"Fine. Rehearsals are going well. Midterms are all over."

"When's the performance?"

"We open a week from Saturday and run through the next weekend."

"Great! I'll be there. I'm being discharged Saturday."

I was delighted. "I'll fix up your room special."

"Don't bother. It's fine the way it is. Uncle Bob may

62

be coming in this weekend to speed my recovery along. Come, I'll show you the flowers he sent me. Roses. They're on my windowsill."

I was mistaken about him, I thought. He's all right, after all. He must have been upset when I phoned him that night. Look how happy he's made Aunt Ruth.

It was a brief visit because Helen was picking me up on her way home from the photographer's. But I promised myself to come again soon.

Wednesday night the phone rang. Dad answered, talked for a minute and then called Mother. "It's your sister. She sounds very upset."

"Okay—coming."

I couldn't hear what she said because she spoke softly; mostly, she just listened. And I was in the other room. I thought, I hope nothing happened to her leg! I put my books down and walked into the kitchen where Mom was sitting at the table talking on the phone. She was saying, "Don't cry, Ruth. Shhhh! You know how he blows off steam. He must have gotten upset about something. Maybe he misses you and wanted to make you jealous." Then she listened again and finally said, "I can't come tonight, Ruth. Visiting hours are over. But I'll be there tomorrow evening, all right? And I'll tell Mitch. He'll spend some time with you when he stops by. Just take it easy and try not to worry. All right? Good night, Hon." And she hung up the receiver. For a moment she said nothing. Then she turned to me and said, as though she couldn't believe it, "Bob has left Aunt Ruth."

9

I took taxi money and cut out after fourth period the next morning. I got there just as visiting hours were beginning so there was no problem about getting upstairs. When I got to her room, she wasn't there. I spotted her at the far end of the corridor, in a wheelchair, gazing out the window. I walked swiftly to her but she didn't even hear me approach. I tapped her on the shoulder.

"Patty! What are you doing here?"

"I cut out of school. I wanted to see you."

"You shouldn't have, Honey!"

"It's okay. I'm not missing anything. Lunch, study period and gym."

She gave me a big long hug. Then she asked, "How'd you get here?"

"Taxi."

"That's expensive."

"It's all right. I worked last summer, so my money's my own to spend any way I like."

Auntie smiled. "Thanks for coming, Baby. I couldn't

bear being alone in my room any longer. So I got the nurse to let me ride around out here."

"Mom told me about the phone call last night."

She was silent a moment before she said, "Let's go back to my room. I don't want to cry out here."

"You want me to wheel you?"

"No. I can wheel myself. Thank you." So I walked beside her.

As soon as we got inside her room, Auntie's face crumpled and she began to cry. I sat on a chair beside her and stroked her hand. "I can't believe it!" she said between sobs. "He called to say he's flying to New York to be with me. He sent me roses. And two days later he calls to tell me he's 'deeply involved' with another woman and he's leaving me."

"That sounds crazy. Maybe he was drunk or something."

"He wasn't drunk. He stopped drinking months ago. He called me back half an hour after we hung up to make sure I understood that he meant it."

"Would you want him back if he asked you?"

She thought a moment. "I keep expecting the phone to ring. That it will be him saying he made a terrible mistake. But he won't call."

"But if he did?"

"He's not going to." After a while she added softly, "It was probably going on for a long time and I didn't want to see. So I kept myself blind and kept telling myself it was nothing. But it wasn't 'nothing.' It was obviously something."

I thought of telling her about my conversation with him the night she went into the hospital, and how

65

nasty he was. And that I thought she was better off without him. But I didn't say anything.

After a while, she said, "You know, I was planning how we'd celebrate when I got home. We'd have a romantic candlelit dinner. He'd buy me flowers, roses like he sent me here. We'd make up. We'd make love."

She looked as though she was forcing back tears. I didn't know what to say to make her feel better. We were silent a good long while. Then she broke it by saying, "I don't understand how I could have been so blind. It meant so much to me to think our marriage was a success—whatever that means. I never felt a success at anything else. So I had to prove something with my marriage."

I was shocked. I always felt Auntie was a success at everything. She was beautiful—the most beautiful woman I knew—charming, interesting—and nice, too. She acted on TV and occasionally in the movies. I didn't know anyone else who did that. She modeled in magazine ads and she had married a handsome actor; I had to say that. He might not be nice, but he was handsome! Auntie dressed in fine, attractive-looking clothes. She knew what colors were right for her and she made enough money to buy an elegant wardrobe. How could she think of herself as unsuccessful? I tried to tell her that, but she didn't agree.

"My career—it's just that! It's a career. It's not art. It's not acting the way I'd like to be acting. What I do doesn't take talent. Just the right looks. I look like a young nurse or someone's girlfriend. That's really ironic, you know? When I can't keep my own husband! I don't even know if I've got talent—serious talent, I mean. I think I do—I feel I could really get inside a character—but I've never had the chance to prove myself. A Hollywood career like mine has nothing to do with the art of acting. I'm no success! What am I a 'success' at?"

I would feel very successful if I had a career like Auntie's. Yet, I could understand her disappointment at not getting bigger and more interesting roles. It seemed to me there was something missing in Aunt Ruth's criteria for success, though. She was a wonderful aunt—and I loved her very much. Didn't that count? Lots of people loved her even if Uncle Bob didn't. Why was her acting so much more important than real life? I wondered.

"In my eyes you're the most beautiful person I know," I said. "I love you."

She looked at me and smiled and squeezed my hand. "Thank you, darling. Of course, you're not prejudiced, are you?"

"No! Honest."

She sighed. "I wish I felt that way. But I can't. I don't."

After a while, her thoughts returned to Uncle Bob. "Would you believe it," she said. "The woman he left me for was a good friend of mine. We worked a lot of the same soaps together. She usually played the good, faithful wife while I was 'the other woman.' That's a laugh, isn't it? You know, I was thinking all last night, trying to figure out when the romance began. Not that it matters now. But I began recalling so many times when we'd be going someplace—for a drive into the country or for lunch—and Bob would say, 'Why don't we invite your friend, the one you're always acting with? I feel sorry for her. She has no boyfriend. She must be lonely.' Or sometimes he'd say, 'I know you enjoy her company.' He'd make it seem he was suggesting it for my sake. And he'd always pretend he forgot her name. And I never suspected anything!''

Her eyes filled with tears, which she made no attempt to hide from me. There was nothing I could do but listen and try to understand what she must be feeling. There was nothing I could say.

"What are you going to do?" I asked, after a while.

She looked surprised. "Just go on living. Get a divorce." Then she added, "Wash my hair and continue living!" And she laughed. "A few days ago when I thought Bob was coming I made an appointment with the hospital beautician to have my hair washed. I haven't been able to wash it since I've been here. I'm beginning to feel grungy, unattractive. So I'm just going to go right ahead, have my hair done and go on with my life."

"Why don't you move to New York?"

"Maybe. I'd like to try live theater. I don't know if I'm ready. I'd like to be where there's no chance of running into Bob. I don't want to see him again."

She closed her eyes and was silent for a very long time but I didn't feel she'd shut me out. Just that she had gone inside for a while. When she finally spoke, it was scarcely more than a whisper, as though she were speaking more to herself than to me. "I may be better off without him. I was always worried when he wouldn't come home. Wondering where he was, what he was doing, who he was doing it with. He'd phone and make up some excuse and I'd always believe him. No. That's not true. I wanted to believe what he was telling me. I tried to convince myself I believed him. But I felt he was lying to me. I sort of knew he was seeing other women, but I couldn't prove it. I didn't want to prove it." She paused, as though thinking about what she had just said. "So now I won't have to worry anymore. I'll have my peace of mind."

It must be awful not to be able to trust the person you love. I couldn't imagine Mother worrying over Dad that way when he stayed late at the hospital. And I was sure he never worried when she worked late at the office. But I felt if I were married or had a steady boyfriend I'd worry all the time that he might be attracted to someone else.

In school the girls were always gossiping about whose boyfriend was dating someone else, and the girls who were going with somebody in college always worried that he might meet another sweetheart at school. Although I would have liked to have a boyfriend, I didn't want my heart broken.

We were interrupted by the appearance of a heavyset woman with a rolling beautician's cart.

"I'm Hazel. You sent for me?" she asked, with a thick middle-European accent. I smiled. She reminded me of a genie appearing magically at the call of the master.

It was growing late. I wanted to get home before Mother, so I said good-bye and left.

10

Saturday morning, Mother and Dad brought Aunt Ruth home. I wanted to go with them but they said there'd be no room in the back of the car with Aunt Ruth, her suitcase, walker, canes and all the stuff she'd accumulated during her three and a half weeks there. So I stayed home and tried to do my homework, looking out the window whenever a car came down our road and jumping up once or twice to run to the door and wait, as though that would speed them home.

It was a little after noon when I heard the tires crunching in the driveway. I ran to meet them.

"Give Ruth plenty of room," Dad said. "I'm going to help her out of the car. The hugs and kisses can wait till she's upstairs and sitting in a chair."

He opened the walker and set it down beside the car and helped her out of the rear seat. She stood shakily in the gravel driveway clutching the bar of the walker. Dad took her under one arm and led her

through the garage to the basement stair. I ran ahead
to open the door while Mother parked the car. I wondered how Auntie would make it up the flight, but she
assured us she could. "It was the last thing I learned
in therapy. I'm okay. Don't worry." She handed the
walker to Dad and very slowly pulled herself up the
stairs using the bannister.

We were all chattering happily during lunch, and
when we quieted down Mother commented on how
tired Auntie looked. She was very pale and had dark
circles under her eyes.

She laughed. "I really didn't do anything to make
me tired. You folks did all the work. Packing for me,
driving me—"

"You've been through a lot, Ruthie. You need plenty
of rest. Now that you're with us, just say if you need
anything. There are three of us here to help you."

"Thanks, Rachel." She patted Mother's hand. Then
she added, "To tell you the truth, I am exhausted.
You're right."

"I'll help you up the steps to your room," Dad said.

"It's all right. I can make it."

"Patty, go with your aunt. See that she's comfortable."

I was disappointed not to have her company for the
afternoon, but I knew we'd be together for the next
few weeks.

At six o'clock, Mother sent me upstairs to wake-
Auntie for dinner. I rapped softly on the door. After a
moment, she said, "Come in."

It was twilight and the room was dark. Auntie

71

smiled when she saw me. She was lying propped up on two pillows. She slid over so I could sit beside her on the bed.

"Did you sleep well?"

"Oh, yes. Very well. But I wasn't still sleeping when you knocked. I've been up awhile. Just lying here thinking. It's so peaceful."

I squeezed her hand. "I'm glad you're home."

"Thanks. Was it you who put those lovely lilacs in my room?"

"I got them yesterday. I thought you'd like them."

"I do!"

She lapsed into silence. I watched the blanket gently rise and sink as she breathed. I wanted to rest my head on her breasts and feel her cuddle me. After a while, I saw a tear trickle down her cheek.

"What's the matter?" I whispered. "What is it?"

"Nothing. I'm just feeling sorry for myself." It was a few minutes before she continued. "It's just that it's Saturday. And Saturday nights Bob and I used to spend together. We'd drive to this little French bistro. In the country. A very romantic little restaurant with thick wooden tables and candles everywhere. We'd spend all evening there eating dinner, holding hands . . . talking . . . or not talking, just being still together. It was lovely. My favorite time of the week. Now he's probably taking Johanna there."

"Don't think about that."

"It's hard not to."

"It must be terrible. But you'll meet someone else."

72

"Right now, I still miss Bob." She was silent a moment and then she burst out crying, burying her sobs in the pillow.

"Shh-shhh! It's all right!" I patted her shoulders. I felt so helpless. I didn't know what to do to make her feel better. I hated Bob.

"I—can't understand—" she blurted between sobs, "how things—how my life—could change so rapidly. One day he sends me roses—says he's coming to see me. Two days later he calls—he's 'deeply involved' with another woman. How could it be? I didn't even see it coming."

"You're better off without him." But even as I said it, I realized it was no comfort.

"I know. I know that—in my head. But in my heart I still want him back."

Mother appeared in the doorway. "Are you girls coming to dinner? How are you feeling, Ruth? Sleep well?"

"Very well. Thanks. But I feel I could sleep another twelve hours."

"You'll get stronger. It takes time. Need help with anything?"

"Thanks. Patty can help me if I do."

I turned on the light so Auntie could see to get dressed. And then I changed the subject. Perhaps sitting at the kitchen table with all of us would take her mind off her sorrow.

"I must look a wreck," she said, reaching for the slippers I bought her. She swung her legs over the side of the bed and pressed down on the mattress to stand. I reached to take her under the arm but she shook her head. "No, don't, Baby. The sooner I start managing on my own, the better."

When we sat down at the table, Dad brought out a chilled bottle of champagne.

"For your homecoming!" he announced as he struggled with the cork. It popped at last, and he filled our glasses.

I watched the tiny bubbles jumping around in my glass as Dad proposed the toast. "To Ruthie's recovery and to the good health of us all!"

Dinner was lively. We were all talking at once. Auntie had a good appetite and I thought I even detected a little color in her cheeks, probably from the champagne. She spoke of her plans about coming to New York.

"Good! You can stay with us!" Dad said.

"The guest room is yours. You know that," Mother said. "You're the only one who ever uses it."

I leaned over and gave Auntie a hug, nearly upsetting her glass of champagne.

"Thanks," she said. "But I want to get an apartment of my own. In the city. It'll be nearer to things. I always thought I'd like to have my own little apartment in Greenwich Village."

"They're hard to find. Why don't you stay with us while you're looking?"

I was disappointed at her reluctance.

"I don't know. I'll see. Thanks anyway. I may not be coming for quite a while. Maybe I'll work the soaps for another year or so and save up. Moving is expensive. But I would like to get away from L.A."

"Just bear in mind that you're welcome here anytime."

"Thanks."

"Shall we finish off the champagne?" Dad raised the bottle to pour seconds.

"No more for Patty," Mother said. "I think she's had enough."

"No, I haven't! I can hold it without getting sick." I hated when Mother acted like she knew what was best for me and she'd start telling me what to do and what not to do.

"You treat her like a baby," Dad said.

"Well, she's my baby. I don't want to see her get sick."

"If she gets sick, she'll know better next time. A little champagne never killed anyone." And he filled my glass.

We sat around the table a while after we finished dinner. Ruth said, "As soon as I get back to California, I want to start divorce proceedings."

Mother said, "Don't be hasty. Maybe it's a passing fancy—infatuation."

"He sounded definite on the phone. He said some pretty nasty things to me"—her eyes began to water but she didn't cry—"which I won't go into. I can't believe he's the same person who claimed to love me so passionately just a few weeks ago. Who kept saying that our match was made in heaven."

"Did you feel it was?" Mother asked.

Ruth thought a moment. "I wanted to. I tried to tell myself it was. But there were so many things . . . that weren't right. I loved him. But it wasn't a good marriage."

I wondered how that could be. If two people loved each other, why should their marriage be anything short of bliss? I was sure that Mother and Dad were happily married. But they were quite different people from Aunt Ruth and Uncle Bob. Auntie, I felt, was bohemian, a free spirit. She was exciting and creative. Nothing at all routine about her. I felt myself much more akin to Auntie than to Mother. I didn't believe I could be happily married either. I'd want to leave him before he left me so I wouldn't be hurt. Seven kids in my homeroom had divorced parents. They lived all week with one and spent weekends and vacations with the other. And two couples on our block were divorced. It seemed to me that getting married meant letting yourself in for a lot of heartache.

The next morning after breakfast, Auntie and I were sitting on the living-room sofa looking out on the front lawn and the lilac bush, which was beginning to show signs of budding. We were also overlooking the brick and cement home of the Richardsons, who had just gotten a divorce.

"Are you sorry you married Bob?" I asked.

She looked surprised. "No—not at all! We shared a lot of beautiful moments. I guess that's why it hurts so much now. But if I hadn't married him I never would have known his love. We did love each other, Patty. At least I loved him . . . and I believe he loved me." She looked pensive. "Only things changed. I don't know why but they did."

I didn't know it then, but life was only beginning to change for Aunt Ruth.

11

Tuesday morning, Auntie had a clinic appointment to have her staples removed. Mother had an important client coming to see her, so she couldn't drive Aunt Ruth. She allowed me to take the morning off from school to accompany her.

"It's really not necessary, Rachel. I can manage. I'll take a taxi and then I'll just be sitting in the waiting room. There's no reason Patty has to miss classes."

"You may need help. Those hospital corridors are endless. If Patty is with you she can hunt up a wheelchair."

"I don't need a wheelchair. I can walk."

"I'd feel easier if she were with you. Missing one day of school won't hurt her."

I decided I'd remind Mother of this next time I had something I wanted to do on a school day.

"All right, if you insist." Auntie winked at me.

When we entered the lobby, she said, "Let's stop off and have breakfast. We've got plenty of time. My appointment isn't until ten. I love eating breakfast out. It always feels like an adventure. The start of a new day—maybe something wonderful will happen!"

I loved Auntie's spirit of fun. It was hard to believe she was thirty-six years old.

I walked her to a counter stool, then folded her walker and stood it in a corner and sat down beside her. We both ordered full-sized breakfasts with extra coffee.

"It's now—with coffee—that I really miss a cigarette," she said.

"It must be hard. Especially when people all around are smoking. This place stinks from it."

Auntie laughed. "I never minded the smell. But now I do. I just try not to think about it. I'm determined not to go back to it."

Then we spoke of other things and eavesdropped on the doctors around us as they discussed their patients and their colleagues. Auntie invited me to the theater with her as soon as she no longer needed the walker. "Probably a couple of more weeks," she said. "And of course, there's that exciting *Our Town* performance I'm looking forward to seeing."

We made plans for outings together while she was still in New York. And then it was nine forty-five and we had to start heading towards the clinic.

The waiting room was stuffy and crowded. There was scarcely any room for Auntie to use her walker, as people's legs extended in the aisles. We registered with the nurse at the desk and walked to the only unoccupied adjoining seats. A man's jacket was on one. We waited for him to remove it but he didn't. Finally, I asked, "Is this your jacket, sir?" He stared at us angrily, then reached over and put it on his lap, muttering under his breath. We sat. Neither of us felt inclined to talk. I gazed around the room. The seats were filled with elderly people, each apparently accompanied by a spouse. They were lined up man-woman, man-woman, man-woman. I wondered if Auntie was feeling bad that Uncle Bob wasn't with her. Her eyes were lightly closed, but I knew she wasn't sleeping. I wondered what she was thinking. Behind those closed lids, she'd withdrawn into her own world.

Most of the patients either read newspapers or stared blankly into space. Hardly anyone spoke. You couldn't really tell which man and woman belonged together. They all seemed like strangers to each other. Only when the nurse called, "Mr. So-and-So" or "Mrs. So-and-So," then, invariably, a couple got up and came forward, one with a cane or a walker, the other trailing mutely behind. In the far corner by an end table sat a girl about my age with a whimpering baby on her lap. She looked tired and careworn and unhappy. I felt sorry for her.

We waited nearly two hours. There was one couple left when we were called. I carried our jackets and followed Auntie into one of the small examining rooms. A young doctor greeted us. "How are you, Ruth? It's good to see you on your feet. How are you feeling?" He motioned her to sit on the examining table and he got a chair for me. I had met this doctor several times before when I was visiting Aunt Ruth

79

in the hospital. He was friendly and cute. I tried to see if he wore a wedding band.

"You came to have your staples removed?" he asked. "Take off your shoes. Let's have a look. Then I'll get Dr. Keith in here."

Aunt Ruth lifted her legs onto the table and sat with them extended as the doctor palpated her feet for the pulse.

"Very good. Very good, Ruth. You've got a fine, strong pulse."

She winked at me. "Thanks, Doctor. I was a little worried because it was beginning to ache again."

"Nothing to worry about. Let me get Dr. Keith. He'll be delighted."

"I didn't know it was still hurting you," I said when he had gone.

"Nothing bad. Nothing worth mentioning." Then she added, "Thank God!" and I could see she really had been worried.

Both doctors returned a moment later.

"Good to see you, Ruth. I almost don't recognize my patients in their street clothes." He shook hands with both of us. "Dr. Solomon tells me you're doing well. Let's have a look."

He bent over Auntie's foot and got that faraway look in his eyes as he felt for her pulse. He kept his fingers on her pulse a long time without commenting. I saw a flicker of apprehension pass over Ruth's face.

"What's the matter, Doctor? Don't you feel my pulse?"

He glanced up at her briefly. "Not yet."

"It was there a minute ago. Dr. Solomon felt it."

"Yes?" He moved his fingers to another position and pressed hard. Ruth's apprehension turned to fear—then panic.

"Don't you feel it?"

"I'm afraid not. Here, you try, Rod."

Dr. Solomon took over. He smiled. "Here it is, Frank."

"Where? I don't feel it. Show me." Dr. Keith placed his finger where the younger doctor indicated. He held it there then shook his head. "No. There's no pulse there. Try again, Rod."

Auntie was trembling, trying not to cry. I stood by her side and held her hand.

"You're right, Frank. It's not there."

"Oh, my God! What does that mean?"

"Shhh-shhh. I'm sorry, Ruth. It means we're going to have to operate again."

Tears streamed down Auntie's cheeks. "Don't cry, Ruth. If that leg can possibly be saved, we're going to do it. I don't understand what happened here. Once the patient gets by the first ten days it's always safe. I simply don't understand it. I've done hundreds of cases like yours and something like this has never happened." He sighed. "I want you admitted immediately. We'll operate tonight. And Ruth, don't worry. You will walk. I guarantee you that." He paused, then added, "They make wonderful prostheses these days."

"You mean—that I might have to lose my leg, Doctor?"

"I don't know. I hope not. But in any case, you will

81

walk." He turned to me. "Will you accompany her to the admitting office? I'll call so they'll be expecting you."

"Can't I go home—and get some things? My toothbrush, some books to read . . ." I could tell she was looking for a way—any way—to postpone what she dreaded.

"No. Your niece can bring you what you need. Or your brother-in-law. But I want you admitted immediately."

We were both stunned as we left the office. Auntie was pale and unsteady on her feet even with the walker.

"How could it be? How could it be?" I knew she didn't expect an answer.

But I couldn't help thinking that if Uncle Bob hadn't shocked her with the news of his affair—with the ending of her marriage—while she was still in her sickbed, this might not have happened.

When we passed the coffee shop on our way to Admissions, it seemed like an alien place. Just a few hours ago we had sat there enjoying the warmth and comfort of a good breakfast. Now Auntie and I walked on in silence to Admissions. It was a quick procedure. They just needed some information from her. Dr. Keith had arranged everything. An orderly came to wheel Auntie in a chair to the blood lab, X ray and then to her room. I accompanied them. I tried desperately to think of something cheery and hopeful to say to Aunt Ruth but everything I thought of seemed false.

This time she shared a room with three other

women. A nurse came and helped her into bed. We drew the curtain and she changed into the familiar blue and white hospital gown lying at the foot of her bed. I hung her clothes in the narrow metal locker against the wall. She was just removing her shoes when the curtain rustled and a deep, throaty female voice called, "Hurry up. They're waiting to take you to X ray."

"I already was x-rayed."

"That was your chest X ray. You're going to Radiology now for an angiogram."

Auntie shuddered. "I had two angiograms just a week ago."

"I know, dear. But the doctor's operating again and he has to be able to see just what's going on."

Auntie sighed. "All right. I'm ready. No sense making a fuss," she said to me. "I'll have to go anyway. I may as well make the best of it."

They wheeled in a stretcher and transferred her onto it, placing a rolled-up blanket beneath her head, and strapped her down. I accompanied the stretcher to the elevator and then down to Radiology so Auntie wouldn't have to wait her turn alone. I knew she dreaded this test.

"Does it hurt much?" I asked.

"Yes." She didn't elaborate and I didn't ask any more questions. She didn't have to wait long. As they wheeled her inside, she tried to smile at me. "In a couple of hours, it will be over. I'm okay." She said, "Don't wait. Go home. Tell Rachel and Mitch what's going on."

"All right. I love you."

"I love you, too, Baby." And the door closed behind her, shutting me out.

Dad was in the kitchen when I came home.

"I know all about it," he said before I could open my mouth. "Dr. Keith left a message with my secretary. As soon as I take something to eat, I'm going back to the hospital. I want to be in the O.R. for this."

"How serious is it?" I asked.

"It's very serious."

I felt myself starting to cry.

"Crying won't help. We're all doing the best we can to save her leg if it's humanly possible. She's got the best man working on her."

"Does Mother know?"

"Yes. She knows. I called her. She has to work late tonight. She won't be home till about eight. Why don't you fix supper and do your homework?"

"I have rehearsal at seven."

"How are you getting there?"

"Helen's picking me up."

The whole idea of rehearsal, of repeating lines spoken by imaginary characters in a make-believe world, suddenly seemed meaningless to me. It wouldn't change reality. Auntie would still be lying there on the operating table being cut open while we were speaking our lines.

I couldn't enjoy rehearsal that night. I kept wondering how Auntie was doing and whether or not the surgeons would be able to save her leg. I couldn't picture her spending the rest of her life in a wheelchair.

"Patty! That's your cue—where are you?"

I missed my entrance. I hadn't been paying attention. And when I did come onstage, I felt estranged from everything that was going on around me. I was not Rebecca, the character I was portraying, nor did I feel like her. I was Patty whose aunt was being cut open in the hospital. It seemed senseless to pretend to be anyone else. But I acted the best I could knowing it wasn't very good.

Rehearsal lasted very late. I didn't get home till nearly eleven. I expected to see Mother and Dad sitting in the kitchen talking. But Mother had gone to bed and Dad hadn't come home yet. Mother left me a note on the table that Dad expected the operation would be a long one so I should not wait up. I could talk to him in the morning.

I was so tired when I got into bed that I fell right asleep. It was still dark when I was awakened by the grating metallic sound of the garage door rolling open. Dad was home. I waited for him to pass my door so I could ask him about Aunt Ruth but I fell asleep again before I heard his footsteps.

Dull, gray morning light seeped into the room. I was awakened by a loud, harsh clattering against the windowpanes; it sounded like someone typing very fast. Through the thick raindrops I could make out the forms of the red maple and the oak in our backyard, both with branches bent, drooping under the pressure of the wind and the pelting rain, their dark trunks remaining upright, strong, unyielding.

I lay back on the pillows and watched the rain.

Blankets tucked snugly beneath my chin, I basked in the coziness of being warm and dry in my own little room with a nice, hot breakfast soon to come. The alarm clock was due to ring in about ten minutes so I turned it off.

I tried to clear my mind. Bits and snatches of yesterday's events, of rehearsal and missed cues, of Aunt Ruth's missing pulse and of her on the stretcher being wheeled through the corridors, of our breakfast together in the coffee shop and of Dr. Keith's intent expression as he felt for her pulse—they were all jumbled together in my head. I heard Mother running the faucets and puttering around in the bathroom and I knew that Dad must be downstairs having his breakfast. He was always the first to leave the house in the morning.

So I put on my bathrobe and went downstairs to talk to him about Aunt Ruth. He was seated with his elbows propped on the table, his chin resting in his palms. His complexion was pasty-looking and he needed a shave. He had puffy little bags and deep, dark circles beneath his eyes. He looked half asleep.

When I came into the kitchen, he glanced up briefly.

"Good morning. Make yourself something hot. It's nasty out there."

"Good morning, Dad. You look beat. Shall I make you some fresh coffee?"

"Thanks. I didn't get any sleep last night. The operation lasted till nearly four o'clock. Then I spoke with Dr. Keith for a while. By the time I got home it was nearly five. I couldn't sleep. I had too much on my mind."

"How's Aunt Ruth?"

Dad looked me in the eyes. "We couldn't save her leg. Dr. Keith tried very hard; he gave it his best shot. But we couldn't do it."

"You mean he amputated?"

"Not yet. He just sewed her up. He'll have to amputate in a few days."

"Does Auntie know?"

"Not yet. I'll have to tell her this morning. I think it will be easier coming from me. But I'm not looking forward to it. Good news a doctor always likes to tell. But when it's something like this . . ." His voice trailed off.

I rinsed the grounds out of his cup and poured us both some fresh, hot coffee.

"Aren't you taking something to eat, Baby?"

"I'm not hungry."

"You can't go to school on an empty stomach. Not on a day like today."

"I'll take a donut," I said, and brought the box to the table so he could take one, too. I watched him as he ate. He seemed to have aged overnight. His hair looked whiter and there were deep wrinkles across his forehead, at the outer edges of his eyes and leading down from the corners of his mouth. I wondered if these aging signs had been there all along and I hadn't noticed them or if they had suddenly become more prominent. I wondered how all this would age Aunt Ruth. Would she come away from it defeated and old? How could anyone withstand the loss of her husband and her leg in so short a time? Most people never have to suffer even one such ordeal, or, if they do, they're at least much older. For Auntie, the losses would be compounded by the almost certain loss of her career. Whoever heard of an actress with one leg?

Dad glanced at the clock and pushed himself away from the table. "I'd like to postpone this morning forever," he said. "But I suppose, the sooner I tell her, the better."

"I'll come to see her after school, before rehearsal. Tell her, so maybe she won't feel so alone."

"I will, Patty. Thanks. Take care now. Have a good day at school. And try not to worry. She's getting the very best medical care available."

I had a hard time concentrating in my classes, because all day I kept thinking about Aunt Ruth and wondering how she was adjusting to the fact that in a few days she would be without one leg.

Aunt Ruth was sitting up in bed, writing in a notebook when I came in. She smiled at me and put down her pen.

"Hi, Cookie. I decided to start keeping a diary. It makes me feel better to get my emotions down on paper. Maybe someday I'll want to remember what I was feeling or thinking about now."

"Did you see Dad this morning?"

"Yes, I did. I think it hurt him almost as much to tell me as it hurt me to hear it. But it didn't come as a surprise. From the moment Dr. Keith couldn't find my pulse I had this awful sinking feeling; a sort of dread hung over me. So when your father told me, I just said, 'I thought so. When will it be?' He said they'd amputate in a few days. They have to wait for things to settle down to find out just where they have to cut. I'm praying it will be below the knee."

"You're going through so much. I admire your courage. But I wish there was something I could do to ease your suffering."

"What's my choice? I cried on and off all morning. But I don't want to live in a vale of tears. I mustn't look back now or dwell on how things used to be. I'm going to have to learn to walk again. And they say it's not too bad—I still have one good leg and if the other's amputated below the knee it's not difficult to walk with a good prosthesis. So that's what I'll do. And then I'll go back to work. No, I wouldn't call it courage, Baby. The only other alternative is to sink into self-pity and let life pass me by. I find that unacceptable."

"You don't even seem scared."

"You didn't see me half an hour ago. Half the nurses on this floor must have been in here trying to console me. I was so—scared. I am so scared—about not being able to manage for myself, about needing people to do for me. About not getting any more work. After all, who would want to cast a one-legged actress?"

I tried to think of something to say, but I couldn't think of anything. Then she said it for me. "But you know what one of the nurses said to me? She said, 'Dearie, you're so much more than your legs. So very much more. You can't let that stand in your way.' "

She was silent awhile, as though listening to the nurse again and trying to draw courage from her. Then she sighed. "But I am depressed. I feel so much right now, I don't know what I'm feeling." She withdrew momentarily, as though refueling her thoughts. "I guess I'm plenty angry." Her face began to crumple but she worked hard to keep from crying. I wanted to hold her but I felt afraid to approach any closer.

"It's not enough I lose Bob—which may or may not be so terrible. But now, my leg! I could live without Bob—believe me—and be happy. But it's like God is trying to see how much He can heap on me before I collapse."

The early April sunlight began to wane. Shadows filled the corners of the room. In the softness of the hour, I wanted to draw closer to Aunt Ruth. This moment with its hint of purple and of lilacs seemed a part of her, as though it belonged only to her. I knew I had to leave soon to rest before the rehearsal and be backstage by seven. How unreal that world seemed now. Her reality seemed to usurp my own, for she was about to pass through something that would leave her permanently changed and I was merely going to play-act.

Auntie tried to make it easier for me to leave. "I guess I'll sort of get used to the idea," she said.

She relaxed back on the pillow and closed her eyes. Talking to me must have tired her out. I gazed around the room and for the first time I noticed all the get-well cards tacked on the bulletin board, three little plants and a stuffed panda on the windowsill and a stuffed teddy bear by her bedside.

"You've got a lot of people rooting for you," I commented.

"I know. I'm really grateful. All my friends are standing by me." She paused; then she said bitterly, "All except two."

She sighed, then changed the subject.

"My friend Clementine called this morning from California. A short time after Mitch told me the news. So I told her and I started to cry. Clem is a very caring person. That's what I like most about her. But she's also a little eccentric. She's involved in all these prayer groups and every night she runs to a meeting where they all pray for people."

"What do they pray about?"

"About anything. Whatever problems a person may have. She says group prayer always works. And she's going to ask them all to pray for me this week. 'You'll see,' she said. 'Something will come up. Right before the operation the doctors will find a way to save your leg. I can guarantee you won't lose that leg. The Lord is merely testing you.' I wish I could believe her."

"Do you believe in God?" I asked.

"Oh, yes. But not in the way Clem believes."

"I don't."

"No? Why not?" She seemed surprised.

"I don't see any miracles going on. I think if He exists at all, He created a pretty rotten, unfair world."

"I agree. Not on the rotten part. Imperfect is more like it. And unfair—yes, you're right, there."

"So how can you believe?"

"I don't know, but I do. It makes me feel better, I suppose."

This was the kind of response I was used to getting from Mom. Whenever I question her about something and she doesn't have an answer, she merely says, "That's how I think" or "That's how I feel," as though that settled the matter.

"Do you believe He's going to cause a miracle to happen to save your leg?" I asked.

"No. I don't." She was silent a long while; then she added, "I guess I do keep hoping, though." After a while, she said very softly, "I believe He will give me the strength to go on and live a good life—and that's a miracle in itself."

"If you're strong, it's because you're strong. Why credit God with your strength? God has nothing to do with it."

She shrugged. I was angry. Didn't she realize that if God existed at all, he'd betrayed her? Just as Bob had done?

Neither of us spoke for a while, and then I noticed Auntie was crying. I felt guilty for having upset her.

"No, no, it's not you," she assured me. "It's just—so much happening at once. One minute I feel strong and then in the middle of everything I start to cry. It's not you, Baby." She reached for me and I came and sat on the bed and we held each other.

After a while she whispered, "It will be all right because I've got people like you in my life. I guess I'm just beginning to realize the meaning of friendship and real love. You—and all those people who are standing by me—you're teaching me."

I was glad we'd stopped talking about God. And yet, I felt, Auntie hadn't stopped. But at least it wasn't God-this and God-that.

I felt her body begin to wilt in my arms. I didn't want to tire her. She certainly would need all her strength. So I said good-bye.

"Come back soon," she said. "Or call me. I miss you when I don't hear from you. I love you, Sweetheart."

"I will. I promise. I love you, too."

12

Tech rehearsals are endless. They start early, end late and most of the time all you do is stand around while the lighting crew positions the lights—should it be a spot or general lighting for a particular scene; do they want a cool or warm effect; should they use blue or amber gels. And in the meantime, it's very warm on-stage from all the bright lights and the actors can't move around or it will confuse the lighting crew. No one really gets into their parts during a tech because every five seconds, the director calls, "Cut! Stop right there!" so the crew can set the lights for that particular moment in the play. As the evening wears on, everyone gets very tired and usually people start to lose their tempers. But I don't care. I love it anyway. I love the feeling of being part of the magic. A whole world is being created on the stage and I am a part of that world. Everything about it fascinates me, from seeing how the magic is created step-by-step to the painstaking work the actor has to do on her own to make her character a reality, to the setting of the lights, the coordination of sound effects, being fitted for costumes and feeling the character come alive as you look in the mirror and see yourself costumed and made up for the part. But most of all, what I love about it is standing on that stage before an audience and pouring out my heart. I can always sense when the audience is with me and then a sort of supercharge of electricity shoots through me. I get a special kind of energy that allows me to surpass myself. It's like flying.

At last, all the lights, sounds and special effects were set. The tech lasted till nearly one A.M. We got a half-hour telephone break so we could all call home and tell our parents how late we expected to be. Some of the kids ran across the street for hamburgers or ice cream. Then we resumed.

I could scarcely function the next morning, I was so tired. But by dress rehearsal in the evening I had recouped my energy.

There would be two dress rehearsals before opening night. There were a few invited guests at these rehearsals, mostly teachers, and they all seemed to enjoy it, so our spirits were very high as we approached opening night.

Helen drove me to the hospital the afternoon of the second rehearsal so I could visit with Aunt Ruth.

"How's my actress doing?" Auntie greeted me.

"Fine. Tomorrow's the big night."

"Yes? For me too."

"What do you mean?"

She pantomimed cutting her leg.

"They're really going through with it?"

"I didn't expect a reprieve. Clementine will be disappointed, but I wasn't expecting it. I'm lucky because the amputation will be below the knee. That makes it a lot easier for walking."

I couldn't understand how anyone in Auntie's position could call herself lucky.

"The only thing is," she continued, "I wish it were over and done with. I can't stand waiting around. I wish it were finished so I could learn to walk and get on with my life."

If it were me, I'd want to hang on to every last moment that I still had my leg. Though I don't know what good that would do.

I felt guilty around Aunt Ruth because that very evening which should be so wonderful for me would be so terrible for her. But she didn't feel that way.

"I'll be thinking about you," she said. "It helps me. I want to hear all about opening night. How have rehearsals been going?"

"Dress rehearsal was good last night." We both fell silent and I was thinking that a week from Sunday night all our performances would be finished. No more rehearsals—no more Rebecca talking to George, sitting on ladders in false moonlight in an imaginary Grovers Corners, New Hampshire. No more relating to Jeffrey and Susan as though they were Mr. and Mrs. Gibbs, my parents in *Our Town*. They would fade back into being Jeffrey and Susan again. It would be the end of looking forward all day to meeting in the auditorium at three o'clock to enter into a make-believe world.

Auntie must have tuned in on my thoughts, because she asked, "What's the next production after *Our Town*?"

"I don't know. It hasn't been announced."

"You'll try out for it, won't you?"

"Of course. But I'll still miss *Our Town*."

"No, you won't. Not once you get into rehearsals for the new play."

"I don't even know if I'll get a part."

"Try out and see."

"I think I heard they may do Shakespeare."

"What's wrong with that? You can do Shakespeare."

"I don't know. It's so complicated. You first have to figure out what he's saying."

"So you figure it out. He created some terrific characters. Really gives actors the chance to show what they can do. I'd love to do Shakespeare."

"Haven't you?"

"No. My work is all these dumb soaps. You know that."

A sudden worried expression crossed Auntie's face.

"What is it?"

"I just remembered. I have to call Rabbi Kunitz."

"Who's Rabbi Kunitz?"

"He's the rabbi who's seeing to the burial of my leg."

"You're burying your leg?" I was horrified. "You mean, in a regular cemetery, with a funeral and all that?"

"No funeral. No services. Just a decent burial with respect. I was reading in a book I have at home that if a limb or major organ is removed, it must not be discarded with the trash. It must be buried with respect; it's a part of the human body. This Rabbi Kunitz, he's from a funeral home. He's going to come and get my leg as soon as it's amputated, and bury it."

"Will you go to the burial?"

"How can I? I'll be here."

It gave me the creeps to think of Auntie's leg buried in a cemetery as though she were dead.

"Every time I think of it I start to cry," she said. "So I just try not to think about it. I've been talking to my poor little leggie all morning, saying good-bye to it." She fell silent a moment. "Bob and I used to play a little game in bed. We'd pretend our feet were our children. Each of my toes was our special little baby. Pinky liked to be played with and petted, Thumbelina liked to eat a lot of ice cream, Ringy liked to get toys. They each had a personality. It's kind of eerie, but now that their daddy left us, they're going to die."

I tried to imagine how I would feel if I were about to lose my leg. If I were about to cross over from the able-bodied world to the disabled. But I couldn't begin to know how it would be. Auntie had so much courage to be facing the unknown so calmly.

Helen was standing in the doorway. Auntie waved. "Come on in!"

"I'm sorry to interrupt. How are you, Ruth?"

"All right. I hear congratulations are in order, Helen. That you're doing a wonderful job in the play. I'm sorry I won't be able to come and see you both."

"Thank you. I hope things go well for you. I'm sorry

98

to have to cut your visit short," she said, "but I really want to get home and take a nap before rehearsal tonight. I haven't slept for two nights."

"Go on, both of you. Rest up," Auntie said. She gave me a quick hug and motioned us towards the door. "I'll be living it with you two!"

13

It was hot and stuffy and very crowded backstage. The girls shared two narrow dressing rooms stage left and the boys were stage right. A long table with low dressing stools lined three of the walls. A large makeup mirror bordered by small bright lights stood upright by each place. Down the center of the room was the costume rack, each garment clean and neatly ironed, ready to wear, with the character's name scrawled on a piece of paper and tacked to a sleeve or a waistband. We all had to brush by the costumes to get to our places at the makeup table. But first, we each checked to make sure we weren't missing any part of the costume. Mine was a royal blue schoolgirl jumper with a starched white long-sleeved blouse. Helen had three separate costumes, one for each act. Most of the other girls wore dark, ankle-length skirts and long-sleeved blouses, as they were playing towns-women and the play takes place at the turn of the century. They wore their hair in upsweeps or buns while Helen wore hers loose and mine was in braids.

Four senior girls were assigned to help us with our hairstyles and our costume changes.

On the door of each dressing room hung a big gold star, and the first thing that struck you when you entered the room was the sweet sharp smell of greasepaint. I loved the scent. The only place I ever smelled it was backstage and, even more than the costumes, perhaps as much as the curtain calls, the smell of the greasepaint meant THEATER!

Ms. Howard and another teacher came in to collect our street clothes and lock them up someplace safe while we were onstage. The cast had chipped in and bought her an orchid wrist corsage for opening night. She looked lovely, and as excited as we all were.

"Patty, I have something for you." She handed me a bunch of delicate red tea roses. "These just came a little while ago." The card read "I know you'll be great! I'll be thinking of you. Love from Aunt Ruth."

"I'll find a vase and put them in some water so they'll keep till after the performance," Ms. Howard said. "You go ahead and get your makeup on."

As I sat down at my place and felt the warmth from all the makeup lights on my skin, I thought of Aunt Ruth. I imagined her making up before going on camera. I knew she was proud of me now just as I always was of her. It brought tears to my eyes when I thought of how her acting career might be ending at the very moment mine was beginning.

I reached for the jar of base labeled "Youth—female" and dabbed some on my forehead, cheeks, nose and chin. It was cool and soft and slightly greasy and it spread easily, imparting to my complexion a slight pinkish hue. I massaged it in evenly all over my face. I no longer looked exactly like me. I started concentrating on the change that was beginning to occur. I was already more my idea of what Rebecca looked like. Susan, who was sitting to my left, was powdering her hair. I would soon be relating to her as though she were my mother. With my pink cheeks and my braids I was certainly more Rebecca Gibbs now than I was myself. Yet, of course, I was still me, only I was beginning to feel like a different me. A me who lived at the turn of the century in Grovers Corners, New Hampshire, and whose life was relatively simple.

"Ten minutes! Ten minutes, please!" There was a flurry of "Ooooh!" and "Aaaah!" and "Wait—I'm not ready!" A lot of the girls spent so much time talking as they made up, talking about ordinary things—their boyfriends, homework, the movies—you'd never know they were getting ready to enter another world. I preferred concentrating all my energy on imagining what it was like in Grovers Corners, New Hampshire, and what it would feel like to be Rebecca Gibbs. I wanted to turn to Susan and address her as Mama and start talking to her the way I imagined Rebecca Gibbs talked to her mother. But I knew Susan would think I had flipped. She was talking with two other girls about a rock group.

"Places, please! Places, everybody! Places!"

My heart began thumping wildly. Mine was only a small role, yet I felt as though the success of the entire production depended upon how well I did it. I could hear Aunt Ruth saying, "There are no small parts,

102

only small actors," and I understood what she meant. My part was very important to the success of the whole.

I found myself a spot just behind the sight lines where I could stand and watch the action until it was my turn to enter the scene. In this play, there is no curtain. Nor is there any real scenery. The audience faces a bare stage until the actor playing the role of the Stage Manager comes on, sets a couple of chairs and tables in place and starts talking to the audience. I prefer plays that do have curtains that rise in the beginning and come down at the end of each act because that makes it seem more like THEATER. But this way is okay, too, I guess. In a few minutes my cue would come. Mrs. Webb and Mrs. Gibbs both summon their children to breakfast. I call from offstage, "Ma! What dress shall I wear?"

Then nothing else matters to me but the reality of the moment—of me as Rebecca Gibbs and of Susan and Jeffrey as my mother and father. And the imaginary Grovers Corners, New Hampshire, as my hometown where I go to school and know everybody and where all my friends are. Grovers Corners becomes the most real place in the world for those two hours of the play. For weeks, I've been thinking about this place and these characters, creating offstage lives for them so that now I am prepared to inhabit their world and to believe in it.

It seemed like no time at all and we were lining up for our curtain calls. The audience was wildly enthusiastic, filled as it was with our families, friends and classmates. I took my bows together with Jeff and Susan. Helen got her own special curtain call and the loudest applause of all. The principal handed her a tremendous bouquet of roses from the foot of the stage. I knew someday I would be taking a solo curtain call and someone would hand me a bouquet of roses. I felt joy and elation—I knew I was an actress!

14

After the performance everyone went out partying: a whole big group went to the pizza joint; some went for hamburgers and Helen and a few others went to Baskin-Robbins. I went with Helen. Mostly, I don't care for partying. Everyone is always talking at once and no one listens to what anyone else is saying. And, unless you're very popular, no one talks to you at all. I prefer being with just one or two friends or a very small group.

I thought about Aunt Ruth when Helen drove some of us home after Baskin-Robbins. I was sorry to end such a wonderful evening though there were still five more performances to look forward to. I got into bed and set the alarm for seven A.M. so I could be dressed and ready to go to the hospital with Dad when he made his rounds in the morning. But when I awoke, the morning sun was long since gone from the room. It had the feeling of late afternoon. I glanced at the clock. It was just four. I got out of bed and put on my robe and went downstairs to the kitchen, where I heard the whirrrrring of the washer and the dryer. Mother was sorting the laundry at the kitchen table.

"Did you have a good sleep? I was going to wake you in another half hour so you'd have time to get ready for tonight and to eat a good supper."

"I'm not hungry." I was feeling grumpy—and angry—because I missed my chance to visit with Aunt Ruth. "Why didn't you wake me earlier? You knew I wanted to go in with Daddy this morning."

"I tried, but you were sound asleep. I decided if you were that tired, you needed the rest. You can see Ruth tomorrow. She's exhausted, too, by the way. She called before. She sends you her love. She's been sleeping most of the day, too, so you don't have to feel so bad. Now, how about letting me heat up some soup for you, or I can heat the fish cakes and spaghetti if you prefer."

"Okay."

"Okay what? Which do you want?"

"Both, please." I felt silly, having just refused to eat. "I guess I am pretty hungry after all." I smiled at her.

As I ate, I waited for Mother to tell me how much she liked my performance last night, but she seemed to have forgotten about it. Finally, I said, "Did you see the play last night?"

She seemed surprised. "Of course, we did. It was very good. You were very cute."

"I don't want to be 'cute.' That's demeaning. I want to be good. Was I good?"

"I'm sorry for using the wrong word. Don't get so

excited. Of course, you were good. You were very good. After all, you're our daughter."

"That's exactly what I mean."

"What you mean about what?"

"Being demeaning!" Then I mimicked Mom. " 'You were very good. After all, you're our daughter.' That says nothing about what you thought of my acting."

"Well, if that says nothing to you, then maybe I better keep my mouth shut."

I was furious. All I wanted was for Mother to tell me that she thought I was really a fine actress—but she wouldn't say it. Was it because she didn't think so or because she was afraid I'd want to become an actress, which I already did—more than anything— but I just didn't talk about it. But if all Mother could do was put me down with words like "cute" and "you're our daughter" I wasn't going to sit there listening to her. So I pushed myself away from the table, spilling some soup in the process, and ran upstairs to my room.

But as soon as I slammed the door, I was sorry. I knew Mother must be very upset about Aunt Ruth and I wasn't helping matters by losing my temper. I needed to talk to someone who would understand. But I didn't want to disturb Aunt Ruth if she was resting. I knew that Mother never approved of Aunt Ruth's career either. Only, since they were just sisters, Mother had no say in the matter. But I knew she disapproved, from the expression that often settled in her face like a dark rain cloud when she spoke about Auntie and her life-style, and from the tone in her voice whenever she used the term "a little bohemian" to describe her sister. I knew that Mother preferred that I become a stockbroker like her or a scientist or even a professor. But these were not for me. I had so many feelings, so much I wanted to experience, but could not in a single lifetime, that the only way was to express it all through the characters created for the stage. It was when I was onstage, even in a small part, that I felt most alive.

I didn't want to call Helen either because I was afraid she'd start telling me of all the praises her parents had heaped on her for her acting—and I just didn't want to hear it.

So I pounded my fists into my pillow until I was exhausted and then I just lay there and thought of nothing.

The performance that evening was a let-down from opening night. Most of the kids seemed to have the attitude that they'd already proven themselves so they didn't have to concentrate anymore. A few of the boys were mumbling jokes under their breath, trying to make the rest of us crack up onstage. But no one did. When Jeffrey, who was supposed to be my father, whispered to me, "Come on, Babe, I'll show you a good time," I became very angry. Not only because he was spoiling the reality of the scene for me, but because I wanted everyone in the play to take it seriously. If all they did was fool around then they, themselves, were demeaning the art of acting and leading the way for other people to look down on it.

108

*   *   *

I didn't get to visit Aunt Ruth until the weekend performances were through. Helen couldn't drive me because she had to study for an exam, so I took a taxi.

Aunt Ruth was sitting in the armchair by her bed with two pillows and a wooden board tucked under her. The board, which was also propped up by the other visitor's chair, was to rest her amputated stump upon and keep it elevated. Her legs were draped with a sheet and a thick white blanket. I was very curious about her stump but was careful not to stare.

Auntie looked up and smiled as soon as I came in. "Patty! I missed you!" Then she laughed. "Don't worry. I'm not the invalid I may appear to be. The physical therapist was in this morning and she's already started me on an exercise program. Leg raises, weight lifting—I have to develop upper body strength for using the crutches. I'll be stronger than ever by the time I leave here."

I sat down in the wheelchair as Auntie was using both regular chairs. I rested my legs on the leg rests and released the brakes so I could maneuver myself a little closer to her. "Hey! This is neat!" I exclaimed without thinking. "It's a great way to get around when you're tired. Beats walking!" Then I noticed the pained expression on Auntie's face and realized what I'd said.

I was relieved when she changed the subject.

"So—how did the performances go? I wish I could have been there. I thought about you."

"Thanks for the beautiful roses."

109

"I'm glad you liked them."

"They arrived as I was getting dressed for the performance. They made me feel so special."

"You are special."

I got up and threw my arms around her. After a moment, I realized I was crying.

"What's the matter? What is it?"

I didn't know why I was crying. Was it for Auntie, thinking how she might never get another acting part, that she might never even walk again? Or was it for myself and my anger at Mother for disapproving of what meant most to me in the world? Or was it an overwhelming relief at finally being with the one person I knew would understand?

"Aunt Ruth, when you first decided you wanted to be an actress, how did your parents respond?"

"I was just about your age. No one took me seriously. They didn't object to my being in school plays as long as my work didn't suffer. They figured I'd 'get it out of my system' that way."

"And what happened when they saw you were serious?"

"They didn't like it. Your mother wanted to be a pianist. She was very talented, too. She majored in music in college, but minored in economics, just as our parents begged her to do. And when she graduated from college, she went right into the financial field. She seemed to forget all about her music. I'll never understand that. She stopped practicing; she scarcely ever sat down at the piano. I once asked her about that. All she said was, 'All that is behind me. There are more important things in life than music and playing the piano.' I never mentioned it again and neither did she. But I felt sad for her. Our parents expected me to do the same. To give up acting and settle for something more practical. And they couldn't understand when I didn't."

"Do you think my mother wanted you to give up acting, too?"

"Oh, yes. She most of all. My pursuing it was a continual reminder to her that she did not have to abandon her art. She chose to. I don't think she still thinks about it, though. I think she's pushed it all into the past."

"I never knew. I never pictured her being a musician."

"She could have had a brilliant career as a concert pianist but she had other goals."

"Being a stockbroker?"

"I mean getting married. Your mother never lived on her own. She lived at home until she met Mitch and they got married. Then she became 'Frau Herr Doktor'!"

"What do you mean?"

"She gave up her own career in order to be Mitch's secretary until he didn't need her that way anymore. My sister has always sacrificed her own desires to please other people."

"I'd never sacrifice my goals for my husband's!" I declared flatly. "Let him sacrifice his for mine!"

"No one should have to sacrifice themselves to please anyone else. That's one good thing I can say

111

for Bob. He never demanded I make my career sub-servient to his. I wouldn't have done it if he did, but he didn't."

"Do you think Dad demanded that of Mother?"

Auntie considered a moment before she said, "I don't think so. But I do think your mother felt he expected it of her. And then again, maybe she felt she wasn't such a good pianist after all and she didn't want to be put to the test. You know your mother. She always tries to do what is expected of her."

"I could never live like that!" I said, not stopping to realize how important it was to me that Mother and Dad should not only approve of my acting, but feel I was good and encourage me. "Are you and Mother still angry at each other then?"

She thought a moment. "No. I wouldn't say . . . I think . . . angry is the wrong word. We still disapprove of each other's life choices. But perhaps that's a thing of the past, too."

It was growing late. Twilight was seeping into the room as a veil between us. I could no longer distin-guish Auntie's features; but the sense of her strength and undaunted determination burned through.

After a long silence, Auntie whispered, "Maybe I said too much—about your mother, I mean. I just want you to understand how important it is to remain true to yourself—and to your dreams and aspirations. Otherwise, you'll always regret it. I'm not saying you'll be miserable—you may lead a very good life like your mother—but somewhere down deep there will always be that little worm of discontent gnawing away."

"Did you ever feel discontented with your own life?"

"Yes; I've been thinking about that a lot these past few days. And I think I'm ready to make a move."

I was sorry I'd asked the question. How could anyone be satisfied in life with only one leg?

But apparently Aunt Ruth wasn't thinking about her leg at all. "I've known for a long time, maybe since the beginning of my career, that what I do isn't quality art. It isn't art at all. It's merely a lucrative career. I've been afraid to admit it to myself—that even though I'm called an actress, I'm really not. Only I've been afraid to leave the commercials and the soaps to try for what I really want to do—live acting—on the stage—before an audience. Those kinds of acting parts are hard to come by, and unless you make it big, a lot of them don't pay at all. Most actors support themselves waiting tables or in temporary office jobs. It would probably mean moving to New York where live theater is—but I've got a nice, comfortable home in L.A. and rent is very high in New York City. I'm afraid I'd go through my savings right away."

"You could live with us!"

Ruthie smiled and squeezed my hand.

"I don't think that would work out too well."

"Why? Because you and Mother wouldn't get along?"

"Because I'm too independent to live for very long under someone else's roof. I need my own place. I need to be able to come and go and to do things my way."

I loved the idea of Auntie moving to New York. "Do you think you really will?" I asked.

113

"Definitely! Now more than ever. I realize how precarious life is—so if there's something I want to do, I'd better get on with it."

I didn't mention it, but I was looking forward to the day when I could move in with Aunt Ruth.

Thursday afternoon, when Mother offered me a lift to visit Aunt Ruth with her, I felt funny about being with them both at the same time. I almost felt as though I had betrayed Mother by listening to what Ruth had told me Monday afternoon. Not that any of it was bad—or even untrue—just that I now knew things about Mother she hadn't wanted me to know or she would have told me herself. A person is entitled to her secrets. And I felt uncomfortable, knowing what Mother had kept hidden from me all these years. But I felt I understood her better, even though she did not wish to be understood this way.

I told Mother I had two tests to study for so I would have to miss going to the hospital with her that night. She looked disbelieving but she didn't say anything.

After Mother left, I went upstairs to my room. I tried to picture Mother passionately playing piano. It didn't work. I couldn't picture Mother passionate about anything. It was hard to imagine her with strong opinions of her own, no less, and deep feelings—except in those instances when she agreed entirely with Dad. He set the opinions in our family whether political, social or economic. Except for me—I had plenty of opinions, only when I'd express them, Dad would shut me up with "Wait until you're an adult and see how fast you'll change your mind." Now I began to wonder if

114

Mother didn't have original opinions, too, once upon a time, only she'd learned to keep them all inside so as not to displease Dad.

Then I thought what Auntie had said about always being discontented if you don't try for what you want. I wondered if Mother was discontented. She seemed perfectly satisfied to me. It was Auntie who expressed lack of satisfaction with her work. Then I thought: What if you do try, you make every effort to succeed at what you want to do—but you still fail? How do you feel then? That's what I was really afraid of. Once, when I was around thirteen, I'd mentioned my desire to be an actress. I still remember how Dad responded. "A million young girls want to be actresses. What makes you think you're better than any of them? You'll wind up being a waitress all your life. Surely, my daughter can do better than that." I never brought up the subject again.

Maybe Auntie wasn't completely satisfied with her career, but at least she was acting. And more important, she was getting ready to strike out for what she really wanted to do!

15

Mother and Dad came to the performance on Friday night. We stopped at Baskin-Robbins for ice cream on the way home.

The phone was ringing as we came into the house. Dad answered it. There were a few brief "Yes?" "Hmmm!" and "How does it look to you?" Then, "I'll be there as soon as I can. I'm on my way now." And he hung up.

Mother and I hadn't taken our coats off yet. "That was Frank Keith," Dad said. "Ruth is having problems with her good leg. Frank can't find any pulse. Her leg turned cold and it hurts. I want to get right over there."

"I'll come too," Mother said. I didn't say anything but just trailed along and climbed into the backseat of the car.

When we reached her room, Auntie was lying propped up on pillows, her eyes round with fear, glancing anxiously from one doctor to the other. She was surrounded by four young interns and Dr. Keith. Dad, Mother and I made eight of us crowded around her bed.

"Let me see that foot," Dad said.

Auntie pulled aside the blankets. "It's very cold," she said.

"That's okay. My hands are cold, too."

Dad held her ankle, then moved his fingers to press on the sole of the foot, and then a little higher up her leg. Everyone was focused on Dad but his expression revealed nothing.

"Do you feel it?" Auntie whispered, scarcely daring to breathe.

Dad palpated her foot a few seconds longer; then he gently set it back on the sheet and covered it. "I don't feel a thing," he said.

"Neither did I," Dr. Keith replied.

"Oh God," Auntie cried softly, searching Daddy's face for some reassurance. "You don't think I'll have to lose this leg, too, do you?"

"I'm sure you won't, Ruthie," Mother said. "Don't worry."

"Maybe you should be the surgeon!" Dad snapped. "I don't feel a pulse. Neither does Dr. Keith. I don't know for sure that she won't have to lose the leg. I hope not. But I don't know. If you know so much, Rachel, that you can assure her, maybe you're in the wrong profession. Maybe you should be the surgeon."

I felt bad for Mother with Dad hollering at her in front of everyone. She was only trying to comfort Aunt Ruth.

"I'm ordering an angiogram for first thing tomorrow morning," Dr. Keith said. "And I'm reserving space in the O.R. in the afternoon."

"For me?" Auntie asked weakly.

"Yes, of course, for you," Dr. Keith responded, walking towards the door. Dad followed him out of the room, the two of them consulting together. The young doctors made a rush for the door, too, only Dr. Keith sent one of them back into the room to start an i.v. on Auntie. Then Mother and I left, too. There was so much I wanted to say to Auntie, but I didn't have the words. So I leaned over to kiss her good-night, but Mother pulled me away. "Don't give her any germs now before her surgery." So I straightened up and smiled to Auntie, though there was nothing to smile at. She returned my smile, made the "V" for victory sign with her fingers, then closed her eyes.

I wanted to go with Dad to the hospital the next morning, but he said it was pointless. "She'll probably be down at Radiology most of the morning. And then, if there's time before the surgery, she should sleep. She'll need all the strength she has."

So I stayed in the house and did my homework until it was time to start getting ready for the evening performance. I phoned the hospital three times to inquire about Aunt Ruth. The first time I was told, "Her condition is satisfactory." I got angry. I felt like saying, "There's nothing satisfactory about possibly losing your only leg! Maybe it's so 'satisfactory' to you, lady, whoever you are, because you plain don't care. You don't give a damn!" But instead I mumbled "Thank you" and hung up. The next time I called, I was told,

"There's no patient here by that name. Maybe you called the wrong hospital."

And finally, just before I was ready to hang up the third time, the operator said, "She's in surgery now. We have no report on her."

The performance went well, though I was worrying about Auntie the whole time. Afterwards, Helen dropped me off at home. Mother had just gotten in the house a few minutes before.

She hugged me when I came in, which surprised me, because Mother was not a physical person. By the length of time she held me and by her silence, I knew she must have been crying, only she didn't want me to know. That's why she wasn't speaking. So I held her around the shoulders and patted her gently. After a while, she pulled back and tried to smile.

"Dad went back to the hospital. Ruth is finished with the surgery. She's in the recovery room. But . . ." Her voice choked.

"But what?" I prompted, already knowing what she'd tell me.

"But . . . they won't be able to save her leg."

"You mean—she'll be a double amputee?"

Mother nodded. "Yes."

My mind filled with the image of a man I had passed on Fifth Avenue regularly when I used to go into the city on Saturday for my ballet class. He also was a double amputee. I used to think of him as the "half man." He would sit on a sort of low wooden platform pieced together from old planks and mounted on roller skate wheels. He never wore prostheses so you could see just where his legs ended under the bent-

119

up flaps of his trousers. Around his neck on a piece of cardboard was scrawled: "Please help me. I'm a cripple. Thank God for your blessings!" And in one hand he held a tin cup containing a few coins which he rattled at every passerby. I always tried not to look at him, but he was hard to avoid as he placed himself right in the middle of the sidewalk. He only reached up to most people's waists because of his sitting on those low boards. And because of his pleading expression whenever he caught someone's eyes and a soft, pitiful whimper he emitted, he seemed more like a wounded dog than a human being. I shuddered now when I thought of Aunt Ruth without her legs.

In the morning, I was dressed and ready to leave with Dad for the hospital. So was Mother. All together, we would try to cheer her up.

Dad related to us how he broke the news to Ruth. "She looked me straight in the eyes and nodded and said, 'I knew it. I felt it.' She didn't break down crying; she just sat there, propped up on her pillows, tears streaming silently down her face. All I could do was give her some tissues."

When we reached the lobby, the gift shop was just opening. We went inside and selected a half dozen magazines to bring to Ruth. And then I spied on the shelf a mug with her name in a neat, curlicued script and a delicate rosebud design, which I bought for Auntie and had gift-wrapped in blue and violet tissue paper. I thought about the slippers I had bought for her in this shop—perfectly useless.

*　　*　　*

"Come on! Wake up—wake up, Sleepyhead! You've got company. You can go back to sleep later." Dad was the first to enter the room. He motioned to us. "Come on, girls, she's decent! Up and at 'em, Ruth!"

Auntie rubbed her eyes and smiled to us. Her face was ashen and she had deep circles under her eyes. Her copper-colored hair, somewhat dulled, tired-looking like the rest of her, spread wantonly on her pillow and down her shoulders.

"I'm sorry I can't sit up," she apologized. "My leg hurts too much to move."

"Stay right there. We can visit with you fine this way," Mother said.

"Mitch, can I have a painkiller, please?"

"If you're asking me—no. You know how I feel about painkillers."

"But it hurts—an awful lot."

"Ask the nurse for some Tylenol."

"That doesn't do much. Not for this kind of pain."

"Sorry. There's nothing I can do for you. A little pain won't hurt you. You know what they say—no pain, no gain!"

"Thanks a lot."

I was furious with Dad for being so flip about Auntie's suffering. Yet I knew he really did care.

Auntie changed the subject. "How's the play going?"

"We only have tonight's performance left."

"Did you enjoy doing it?"

"I loved it!"

"Good!" Auntie sighed. Her eyelids dropped. She

seemed too weary to continue. "Have they decided yet what the next production will be?"

"I think we should let Aunt Ruth rest now," Mother said. "We'll continue the conversation some other time."

Auntie hardly seemed to notice our leaving. I couldn't help wondering how she felt about this theater talk. Surely, her own career was ruined. An actress must be able to walk well, move gracefully, perhaps run or dance or climb stairs or bend down to pick up a child, if the role calls for it. Auntie would be lucky if she learned to walk with crutches—if she ever walked at all.

Later, after the performance, a lot of us were crying. It was sad to leave the imaginary town of Grovers Corners, New Hampshire, we'd inhabited all these weeks. Sadder still, for me, was divorcing myself from the character of Rebecca Gibbs, who would now slowly fade from my life.

We all pitched in to clear the stage, clean the dressing rooms, hang the costumes. A lot of us had decorated the dressing-room walls with our favorite photographs, pictures and even some posters. All these had to be removed now to leave a clear area for the cast of the next production.

A few boys who weren't in the play came to help, among them Roy, the ex-boyfriend of the most beautiful girl in the school. They pretended to ignore each other but I could tell they weren't. Emma kept glancing at him and straightening her clothes and Roy kept grinning. I wondered how it would feel to have a boyfriend who cared enough to pursue me even after we broke up. I wondered why they had split up. They always used to hold hands in the halls, and they looked so good together they were voted the "best-looking couple" in the senior yearbook. I wished I had a boyfriend like Roy.

There was a lot of anxious speculation as to what the next play might be. "It will be posted Wednesday morning on the drama bulletin board," Ms. Howard announced. "So if you'd like to try out, be prepared to stay late Wednesday, Thursday and Friday afternoons. I'm hoping the casting won't take more than three days."

A few of us tried to get her to reveal the play so we could read it and practice before the audition.

"I'll only tell you what you already know," Ms. Howard said. "It's by Mr. William Shakespeare. I can't tell you any more or it wouldn't be fair to the others."

I went to bed early Tuesday night so I'd be well rested for the audition. But I was so nervous I couldn't sleep. I kept thinking about performing and about Aunt Ruth. I wanted to find a way to include Auntie in the excitement so she wouldn't feel left out. I decided to phone and ask her advice about the auditions.

"How are you feeling, Aunt Ruth?"

"Not too bad, considering . . . but how are you? Tomorrow's the Big Tryout, isn't it?"

"Yes. And I'm really nervous."

"No sense letting it get to you now," she advised. "There's nothing you can do about it. You don't even know which play they're doing. Only tomorrow, when

123

you try out, concentrate fully on what you're saying and doing. Don't let your mind wander and don't worry about characterization. Just try to believe in what you're saying."

"I'll try."

"I know my telling you not to worry won't help much. I always worry a lot before an important audition. But, believe me, it does no good."

I still didn't sleep well that night, though talking with Auntie made me feel better.

As I was drifting off to sleep, I half imagined, half dreamed I was at the auditions and, instead of Ms. Howard directing, it was Aunt Ruth. She sat in a wheelchair, like a throne, on the stage and whenever she wanted to direct, she stood up and walked across the stage. As she returned to her chair, she winked at me.

I kept checking the drama bulletin board between all my classes Wednesday but it wasn't until after fifth period that the notice went up: CASTING CALL FOR SHAKESPEARE'S ROMEO AND JULIET IN THE AUDITORIUM AT 3:00 P.M. My heart fluttered and I began trembling. I wanted to play Juliet! I thrilled at the thought of it—and then panicked. I had to not only be good—I had to be the best! I thought of what Dad once said to me. "A million girls want to be actresses. What makes you think you're any better than they are?" And my heart sank. There'd be a lot of would-be Juliets auditioning for the role.

I passed Helen in the corridor on my way to class.

"Are you trying out?" I asked, hoping against hope that she was too busy.

"Of course! Now that I've gotten a taste of acting, I really like it. You bet I'm trying out!"

There goes Juliet, I thought to myself. Maybe I'll get a minor role.

I was the first one in the auditorium at three o'clock. I tried to wait patiently for Ms. Howard, but I was jumpy. I kept picturing myself in the balcony scene in a satiny white evening gown.

In a couple of minutes, the rear door banged open and a gaggle of girls, chattering like geese, flew down the center aisle to the front row where I was sitting. Among them was Emma. If the role were to be cast on looks, she would surely get it. Next, a few boys from the *Our Town* cast came sauntering down the aisle. When Ms. Howard entered through the front side door, carrying a stack of paperback *Romeo and Juliet*s, and piled the books on top of the piano, my fingers turned to ice and I began to tremble. Oh, please, please! Let me be Juliet!

Ms. Howard distributed the books and then wrote the numbers of the scenes she wanted us to read on the blackboard in the corner of the stage. I jotted them down on a scrap of paper and then took my copy of the play to the rear of the auditorium so I could read the scenes and practice undisturbed. But it was hard to concentrate as lots of kids were coming through the rear door and down the aisle to the stage. And I was afraid Ms. Howard wouldn't notice me sitting way back there. So I moved to the front again. I noticed Helen enter and take a seat in one of the side sections. She seemed very self-assured.

Ms. Howard passed around sheets of paper for us

125

to print our name, homeroom and home phone number. Then she started calling on some of the boys to come onstage and read a scene. She listened to them for about twenty minutes before suddenly switching to a scene between Lady Capulet, Nurse and Juliet. She called on four or five groups of girls before she called my name. "Patty, I want you to read Lady Capulet." Lady Capulet! I didn't want to read for Juliet's mother! I wanted to do Juliet. But she didn't give me a chance in that scene. A couple of the girls read Juliet very well. She switched back to the boys for a while and then she announced, "Act two, scene two, the balcony scene." All the girls sat forward in their seats, eager to be called.

"Emma, let's start with you. Don, will you read Romeo?" I held my breath. Emma was so pretty that if she gave a halfway decent reading she'd probably get the part. But much to my relief, she didn't put any expression into it. After a couple of minutes, Ms. Howard interrupted. "Thank you very much. Helen, I'd like you to read Juliet. Don, stay up there please and read Romeo with Helen."

Helen sounded flat, too. It was probably just nerves—but I was glad. I know it's not nice—being glad your best friend doesn't do well—but I wanted that role so much.

Ms. Howard called upon a few more couples to read that scene. Then she said, "All you girls sound as though you're looking for a little lost puppy dog when you ask the question, 'Wherefore art thou Romeo?' That's not what it means! He's not lost. What she's saying is, 'Why, oh why, are you Romeo, member of

126

my enemy-family?'' Please try to keep that in mind, anyone else who reads that scene.'' But she didn't call on me anymore that day.

The next afternoon, I did get the opportunity to read for Juliet in three separate scenes. I felt I had done very well, but there were two other girls who also read well and they were both prettier than I. I kept thinking of what Dad said to me. ''A million girls want to be actresses. What makes you think you're any better than they?'' It made me want to cry. That remark put me down to zero; it made me feel like nothing.

I wanted to visit Aunt Ruth and ask her to practice with me and even more to share with her how much I wanted the role and how afraid I was that I wouldn't get it. But there wasn't time. Readings ended at six thirty and I'd have to go home first to get taxi money. Then Dad would probably insist that I stay home to do my homework. And Mother would want me to eat supper. I tried to phone Auntie before I went to bed, but the switchboard wouldn't put through calls to patients after nine P.M.

Friday afternoon, we were all so excited that Ms. Howard had trouble quieting us. Everyone was trying to predict who would get the lead roles. I didn't hear my name mentioned once. I guess no one thought I did well enough. A few of the girls predicted that Marge Hamilton, a senior with professional acting experience, had won; a couple more thought Helen had gotten the part. I wished I could be either of them. We auditioned until nearly seven o'clock and then Ms. Howard announced that callbacks would be posted on the bulletin board Monday morning.

I didn't know how I could stand the suspense that long. On the way home Helen and I stopped in the bookstore and we each bought our own copy of *Romeo and Juliet.*

"I don't really care about Juliet," Helen confided in me, though I doubted she was telling the truth. "The part I really want is Nurse. She gets all the laughs."

"Yes, but Juliet is more emotional."

"You mean melodramatic."

"I don't think so. Her feelings run very deep."

"I still like Nurse. You'll probably be cast as one of the girls in the ballroom scene. I think you'd look good in an evening gown."

"But they don't have any lines."

"I know."

Was Helen saying that I was all right to decorate a ballroom scene, but not to have a real role?

"There's no sense speculating. We'll find out soon enough," I said, trying to sound as though I didn't much care.

I stayed up very late reading the entire play and imagining how I would do Juliet. When the alarm rang at seven A.M., I was groggy. I wanted to pull the covers over my head and stay in bed, but I had to get up if I wanted to go to the hospital with Dad.

Auntie had just finished washing and was putting on her makeup when I arrived.

"Hi, Sweetheart!" She smiled and blew me a kiss. "Pull up a chair. Make yourself comfy. I'll be finished in a minute. I decided to make up and comb my hair every day. It makes me feel more a part of the world.

Like I'm on my way to recovery." Then she asked, "How are the tryouts going?"

"She's posting callbacks Monday."

"Expect you'll be called back?"

"I hope so. I bought a copy of the play. I was wondering if you wouldn't mind practicing with me."

"I don't think you should practice anything because you don't know what kind of interpretation the director will want. But why don't we read through some scenes together for the meaning?"

We went through the play, reading aloud every scene where Juliet had lines. We were near the end when Dad interrupted.

"Don't tire your aunt like that, Patty. She needs to rest."

I had been so anxious about the auditions, I hadn't noticed how tired Aunt Ruth looked.

"It's all right, Mitch. I don't mind."

"I'd rather see you resting. You've been through an ordeal. You need plenty of rest for proper healing."

I was beginning to feel guilty. But Auntie glanced from me to Dad and back to me again. "It's all right, Mitch. It takes my mind off the pain. I like it!"

"The last thing you need is an infection or pneumonia. You're very vulnerable. Doctor's orders. I want you to rest now."

"I'm tired of reading these scenes anyway," I fibbed.

"No, you're not!" Auntie chided. "But you're a dear for making things easier by saying that. Maybe after lunch if you're still around or if you can come back again we can read some more."

"Thanks, Ruth. That's very kind of you. I hope Patty

appreciates how good you are to her. But I want her to stay home this afternoon and do her homework."

I hated when Dad answered for me. And I got very angry when he said that about my appreciating Auntie's goodness. Of course I did!

I got to school early Monday morning and raced to the bulletin board just outside Ms. Howard's office, but nothing was posted yet. I hung around a little while hoping Ms. Howard would come by with the callbacks, but she didn't. A few of the other kids, including Helen, also stopped by and then drifted off to class, seeing that there was no news. After a while, I had to go, too. But after first period I checked the board again. Still nothing. After second period, as I approached the bulletin board, I saw a whole group crowded around it. Helen was in the center, right up close by the board. I pushed my way close enough to read the announcement. My name was among those on the callback sheet, along with Helen's. There were about a dozen names listed from all those who had auditioned. There was a lot of excited conversation. Those who weren't listed just turned and walked away. "I didn't care anyway," I heard one girl remark. "Shakespeare's not exactly my cup of tea," one of the boys added. But among those of us who were selected, we were trying to guess who was being considered for which role.

At three o'clock we were all in the auditorium awaiting Ms. Howard. I was so nervous I had a stomachache and my hands were icy. Finally, Ms. Howard arrived. She called upon us two at a time to go up on the stage and read some of the key scenes. I read opposite three different Romeos. I felt I'd done well, but there were two other would-be Juliets who also read well.

"Thank you all very much. You all did a good job. We'll be rehearsing every afternoon plus occasional evenings and Saturdays. Does anyone have a problem with that?"

No one raised a hand.

"Good. I'll have the casting posted tomorrow sometime after fourth period. And we'll have our first complete read-through at three o'clock here in the auditorium. See you then."

I raced to the phone to call Aunt Ruth. "Do you think I got it?" I asked.

Auntie laughed. "I really don't know, Patty. But I'll tell you one thing. You must have been very good to have been called back. Don't forget that. Ms. Howard may have some physical type in mind or she may be trying to pair off a Romeo and Juliet who look good together. So don't worry if you don't get the role. It doesn't mean you weren't good." I wanted a more enthusiastic response. As it was, I felt she didn't think I got the part and was just trying to let me down gently.

Mother and Dad surprised me. They both seemed glad I'd been called back. But Dad warned, "Even if you get the starring role, I'll still expect you to keep up with your schoolwork."

Tuesday. Fourth period. I could scarcely wait for the bell to ring. I trembled with nerves every time I thought of the bulletin board and the notice to be posted. Finally, class ended. I made my way through the hordes of pushing and clamoring schoolmates upstairs to the drama bulletin board. I half didn't want to read the notice for fear of the disappointment. But before I even reached the board, someone called out, "Hey, Patty! Congratulations! You're Juliet!" And there it was, clear as day, on the bulletin board. Opposite "Juliet" was my name!

16

We were two weeks into rehearsal. All we were doing at this point was reading through the play and breaking down each scene to make sure everyone understood the language. Ms. Howard explained the background to us—what it was like living in an Italian city-state during the Middle Ages. In those days, the parents decided whom the daughter should marry and a young girl didn't dare defy her mother and father. How different Juliet's life was from Rebecca Gibbs' in *Our Town*—and both so different from my own! But acting was affording me the opportunity to experience both of these girls' lives and still be myself. I was determined to devote myself to acting and the theater.

It was school intersession preceding the final quarter. We still rehearsed every afternoon, but I was free in the mornings so I could visit with Aunt Ruth more often.

One Friday afternoon, Ms. Howard called our attention to a notice she'd posted on the bulletin board.

The White Plains Summer Stock Company was offering apprenticeships to qualified high school juniors and seniors. It seemed very reasonable to me. For only six hundred dollars they were giving daily classes in acting, voice and movement plus the opportunity to work backstage on sets, props, costumes, sound and lighting, plus—and this was the biggest plus of all—the chance to audition for all the plays. It seemed too good to pass up.

Mother and Dad and I had discussed my summer plans earlier. We decided I'd work in an office, live at home and save money for college. It seemed so dull now. I couldn't wait to tell them my new plans for summer stock. But Mother and Dad didn't share my enthusiasm.

"We don't mind paying for your tuition, room and board when you go to college," Dad said. "But you're also going to need books and you'll want nice clothes and you'll want to go to the theater and go out with your friends; all that is extra. That's your share. And it's expensive; don't kid yourself. So if you want to have money, you better start saving. And summer stock isn't the way to do it."

"I don't care about college!" I said. I hadn't really given it that much thought as it was still more than a year off. "I want to be an actress! I never heard of anyone being an actress in college."

"There's a lot you haven't heard of. But I'll tell you one thing. Whether you go to college or not is your decision. But your mother and I pay for your living expenses just as long as you're still in school, whether it's high school, college or graduate school. But after that, you're on your own. We're not paying your way through acting school and we're not supporting you as you seek a career in the theater!" I was disappointed and angry.

"You can't tell me how to live my life! It isn't fair!" I turned to Mother, who had kept silent all this time. "Why don't you say something, Mother?"

Mother spoke very quietly. "Your father already said what needs to be said. He speaks for both of us. We've discussed this many times. We both want to pay for you as long as you're still getting your education. But after that, we feel you should earn your own way."

"But an education in theater is an education!" I argued.

"If you want to major in drama in college, that's another story. But if you're just going out there to take acting classes and go to auditions and live the life of a bohemian—you pay for yourself."

"You're just like Juliet's parents! You're still living in the Middle Ages! They tried to force her into a marriage with someone she didn't love and prevent her from marrying Romeo. And you're trying to prevent me from doing what I want! It amounts to the same thing!"

Dad shrugged. "All right. It amounts to the same thing. So sue me!"

I ran to my room and slammed the door and threw myself on the bed, crying. I needed an ally. Surely Aunt Ruth would stick up for me. It was too late to visit her now, but I decided to ask her in the morning. As I thought about how I would ask her help I began

135

to wonder if she would feel sad remembering the days when she was starting her career. Perhaps I should leave the matter go for a while.

When I got to her room in the morning she wasn't there. The nurse directed me to the gym in the basement where Ruth was having physical therapy.

The sign over the door read "Rehabilitation Medicine." The gym was claustrophobically small compared with the one at school. There were no windows, and a slight sweaty smell permeated the air—not enough to be sickening but enough to let you know that here were human bodies struggling and straining to strengthen themselves, bodies for whom the simplest physical act required great effort.

Mostly there were old people in wheelchairs practicing leg raises or exercising their biceps by stretching thick strips of elastic or by raising and lowering their arms with padded, lightweight mitts wrapped securely around each fist.

As I entered, I passed an elderly woman in a bright blue bathrobe taking mincing steps with her walker. A young therapist close at her side was encouraging, "That's right, Mrs. Samuels, that's good." The rear wall was all mirror. In front of it was a set of horizontal parallel bars about twenty feet in length. Aunt Ruth in her wheelchair was at one end of the bars. Attached to each stump, which was still encased in white plaster, was a steel rod with a wooden shoe. Were these going to be her new legs? They looked like something you'd see in a science fiction movie about creatures invading the earth.

Three therapists were trying to help Auntie to stand.

One held her under the arms; someone else supported her hips and another stood in front ready to catch her, if need be. I watched from a distance. She pulled herself upright by the parallel bars with the aid of a therapist but she was very unsteady and her face twisted in pain.

"Please—let me sit!" I heard her beg.

"Not yet. You think we stood you up like this just to have you sit right back down? I want you to stand for at least a minute."

"I can't—it hurts! Please!"

"Sure you can. You've got to get used to bearing weight."

"Oh, God! How much time do I have left?"

"Thirty-five seconds."

"I'll never make it."

"Sure you will. Straighten up. You're all bent over."

"How much time?"

"Don't worry about the time."

"I never appreciated what a blessing it is just to stand—without pain."

"You'll get there."

I felt ashamed of myself when I thought of the fuss I'd been making over my plans for the summer. My problems were nothing compared with Auntie's struggle to learn to stand again. If it was so painful just to stand, how would she ever be able to walk? What would become of her acting career? What would become of her life?

I watched as they sat her back down in the chair. Her shoulders sagged; her head slumped forward.

"You worked hard!" one of the therapists said.

"You did very well. Tomorrow we'll try for two minutes."

Auntie groaned.

"And by the end of the week I want to see you taking steps."

"You think it's possible?"

"Sure, it is!"

"Then I'll do it!"

I wanted to applaud. I ran up to Auntie and threw my arms around her.

"Sweetie! Where did you come from?"

"I went upstairs to your room but the nurse told me you were here. I watched you stand. You were terrific! I'm so proud of you." I realized I was crying. Auntie held me close. There were tears in her eyes, too.

"You've got—so much courage! I wish I were like you."

"It's not courage, really," she said slowly, as though considering each word. "I'm just doing what I have to do . . . in order to lead the kind of life . . . I want."

The therapist interrupted. "Don't you have O.T. now?"

"What's O.T.?" I asked.

"Occupational therapy. It's where they teach me balance and develop my upper body strength. You want to watch?"

"Sure." I got behind the wheelchair and pushed Auntie through the corridor into the O.T. room. It looked like a kindergarten for grown-ups. There was a long table where people were working with clay and simple weaving projects and crayons with coloring books. On another table were two large upright peg-boards with cardboard boxes of multicolored pegs, and in the rear, two women were playing catch with an oversized beach ball.

There was a child of about three or four in the tiniest wheelchair I had ever seen. He was trying to fit pegs into their proper holes in a board with the help of a therapist. From the back of his oversized skull protruded two tubes.

"What's the matter with that boy?" I whispered to Ruth.

"I think he's had some kind of brain surgery. For water on the brain or something like that. He's retarded, mentally and physically. He's eight years old."

How terrible to have to go through life like that, I thought. Auntie and I watched in silence as the boy struggled with the pegs, obviously not understanding that he had to match each peg with the size of the hole. Finally, in frustration, he shoved the board and all the pegs within his reach to the floor. The therapist scolded him and he flew into a tantrum, screaming and throwing everything within reach—crayons, clay—and crying for his mother.

The therapist was firm, but not unkind with him.

"Your mama isn't here, José. I'm taking care of you now. And I want you to pick up everything you threw on the floor. I'll help you."

Auntie turned to me. "Seeing the other patients and what they have to deal with makes me grateful for my own possibilities of recovery."

A young woman approached us, smiling. "How do you feel today, Ruth?"

"I'm okay. A little exhausted. I stood up for a full minute in P.T. today."

"I know. I heard. Word travels quickly. That's terrific! You'll be walking in no time. Are you up to some balance work?"

"Sure."

Angie, the therapist, led the way to the mats in the back of the room. Aunt Ruth wheeled herself and I trailed behind, trying to observe everyone and everything I could. Trying to incorporate it all into myself—the frustrated little boy with the pegs, an elderly stroke victim whose whole left side was paralyzed and who was trying to learn to butter a slice of bread and cut her food with only one hand, a young man who was learning to feed himself, a middle-aged woman practicing how to tie her shoelaces—all victims of some terrible illness or accident, and all struggling to master the skills needed to live in the world.

I felt struck with my own good fortune—that I had all these skills without effort. I never had to think about tying my shoelaces or buttering my toast. How could people ever get on with life if each and every movement required practice and planning?

As I watched Auntie hip-walk from her wheelchair across the boards to the mat, and then learn to balance while reaching for a large ball thrown too far to her right and then to her left, I wondered how she'd be able to endure all the practice and hard work ahead of her that she needed to master if she was ever to return to her life as an actress.

Aunt Ruth was exhausted after her session. I volunteered to wheel her back to her room so she wouldn't have to wait for the orderly to take her. She was nodding in her chair. When we got upstairs, I held the chair and watched as she hip-walked across the amputee boards into bed and sank wearily back on her pillows. She was asleep in no time. I would have to wait to talk to her about summer stock. I tiptoed out of the room and headed for school and rehearsal.

Ms. Howard was a few minutes late. Sitting in the auditorium with the other cast members, listening to them joke and talk trivia, I couldn't stop thinking about the boy with the tube in his skull and the old woman who was learning to butter her bread—and about Auntie hip-walking into bed. Auntie, missing a major part of her body, but still determined to go on with her acting and her career. How difficult life was! Was it just that way for an unfortunate few, or would we all get our hard knocks with time? My schoolmates seemed to think that life was nothing more than having a good time—a lark! But then my thoughts turned to Juliet and how she learns the heartbreaks of life. I could use what I'd experienced that morning to make Juliet more real.

Someone slipped into the seat beside me. There are plenty of empty seats, I thought. Why does he have to choose this one? I wanted to slide over a seat or two to show I wanted to be left alone. But I knew that would be rude.

"How are you enjoying rehearsals?"

It was Roy Hamburger, alias Romeo.

I didn't want to seem unfriendly—not to Roy. I liked him from the day we met, at the auditions, though we hadn't spoken until this minute. That is, we'd spoken a great deal as Romeo and Juliet—but not as Roy and Patty. He seemed like a gentle boy, even shy, perhaps. He was serious and polite, never horsing around with the other kids. And he was very good-looking. He looked at me intensely during our scenes together. His eyes seemed to widen and change color from blue to gray to green and then to blue-gray; sometimes there were even flecks of brown. He looked as though he wanted to own every word I was saying, that he wanted to possess me entirely. Of course, that was the Juliet-me and he was playing Romeo. We had only spoken to each other in the words of William Shakespeare and within the context of the scenes.

I wondered if he had been the same way with his ex-girlfriend, Emma. Would he be that way with me if I weren't playing Juliet? Had he wished that Emma would get the role instead of me? Thinking about it made me jealous.

"I love the rehearsals. Don't you?" I replied.

"I enjoy them more than the actual performance. They're more relaxing. You're free to experiment and try different things. You don't have to worry so much about making a mistake."

"That's what frightens me about doing Shakespeare. If you forget a line, how do you fill in?"

He grinned. "In our scenes together, I guess we could just start kissing."

He looked right in my eyes when he said this. I felt myself grow warm; I knew I was blushing to the roots of my hair.

"Seriously," he said, "I don't know. That's what I worry about, too."

Then we were both out of things to say. I was afraid he'd move away, so I asked, "Do you want to run lines?"

"Nah! Let's just talk. I don't believe in running lines until I've got enough rehearsals under my belt to know where I'm heading with a scene. Otherwise, it can be damaging. You start to sound flat."

I wondered how he knew all this. He hadn't been in the last production and I couldn't recall running into him at any of the past casting calls.

"Have you acted a lot?" I asked.

"Not as much as I'd have liked. Two seasons of stock and a couple of walk-ons in films."

"I didn't know you were a professional."

He laughed. "I'm not. Yet. I don't have my Equity card. But I plan to get it this summer by doing my third season of stock."

I wanted to know more about joining Actors Equity but Ms. Howard came in. The rehearsal started.

Roy began sitting beside me during rehearsal breaks when neither of us was onstage. Every time I saw him headed in my direction, I grew excited and felt myself flush.

Helen cornered me during class change one day. "You better stay away from him," she warned. "He has a girlfriend. He's going with Emma."

"I don't go after him," I said. "I can't help it if he comes over and sits next to me, can I?"

She shrugged. "Okay. Don't say I didn't warn you."

I had seen him and Emma together a lot during the semester but now it bothered me. Not that he asked me out; he never even asked for my phone number. But when we talked and he looked at me with those beautiful blue-green-gray eyes, I felt mesmerized. I wanted to have him hold me close against his body, not in a rough way, but something soft and gentle. I tried to show how I felt through Juliet and the way I played our scenes together.

Class break ended Wednesday so I couldn't get back to visit Auntie until the weekend. And then it was with Mother and Dad. So we just talked about general things and about Auntie's progress.

"I got my left prosthesis yesterday," she said, "and my right one will be ready in a week."

"How does it fit?" Dad asked.

"It's so tight it's painful. It's a struggle to get into it. I shudder when I think about having to put them on every morning and wear them all day."

"Your stumps will shrink," Dad said. "Then you'll be more comfortable."

Auntie looked skeptical. "I hope so."

I thought it was uncomfortable enough when shoes fit tight—imagine having your legs fit tight!

I was dying to get Auntie's opinion on summer stock and to tell her about Roy, but I didn't dare to mention anything in front of Mother and Dad, and I was still afraid of making her feel bad.

After a moment, Auntie changed the subject. "Guess who I heard from last night?"

"I don't know. Who?" I asked.

144

Mother and Dad looked blank.

"Your and my favorite Uncle Bob."

"What did he want?"

"Just to tell me that he's sent out the divorce papers and expects me to sign them immediately."

"He's divorcing you—on what grounds?"

"I guess on the grounds that he's found another woman."

"The bastard!"

"Patty!" Mother didn't approve of my using certain words even when they were appropriate.

"What are you going to do?" Mother asked.

"I'll countersue. I want a divorce, too. But there's nothing much I can do from the hospital. I'll have to get a lawyer. I want to keep the house. I'll need some-place to live and he's moved in with her anyway."

Then she groaned. "I'm not looking forward to the hassle of a divorce. I've got enough to contend with learning to walk and getting back into life again."

She stopped talking a minute and her eyes filled with tears. "He said—he said"—her voice cracked—"he'd done some reading about my various physical ailments and he knows—I'll be dead in a couple of years—and he'll be glad." Then she broke down com-pletely. "I don't understand—how one day he can swear our match was made in Heaven—then sud-denly wish me dead. It doesn't make sense!"

"These things seldom do," Dad said. "He's found another woman and he wants you out of the way, that's all. It happens all the time."

"I know—but—I still feel terrible that he loves someone else rather then me. Not that I'd want him

145

back even if he changed his mind. I just—don't understand how he could have turned on me like that."

"It happens," Dad said.

"Yes. Obviously it happens. It happened."

I knew I couldn't mention my summer stock problem. Auntie had too much of her own to deal with.

17

I was relieved when Monday came and my day was filled with classes, rehearsals and homework, taking my mind off Auntie. I felt weighed down by her struggles, emotional and physical. I loved her, and I felt totally helpless. There was nothing I could do to help her walk or to make things all right between her and Uncle Bob. I didn't want to think about it anymore. It frightened me to realize that one day I, too, would be grown up and have to face adult problems.

The role of Juliet was a haven for me. As long as I was in the role, either practicing by myself or rehearsing with the others, nothing could happen to me that wasn't in the script. I knew that Romeo would love me till death did us part.

Monday we had a complete run-through of the play although opening night was still weeks off. Helen waited to walk home with me after rehearsal. We hadn't seen much of each other lately because she was only in the grand ball scene and the crowd scenes, and after they rehearsed those, she would leave, never staying to see how the rest of the play was going. Sometimes I felt she was avoiding me, but then, I knew she had homework and other things to do so why should she wait for me?

"Guess what?" Helen greeted me. "I'm going to summer stock! I've been accepted as an apprentice in the White Plains Company."

Suddenly, my role as Juliet didn't seem so important. After all, it was only a high-school production. And Helen would be acting in a regular professional theater this summer. I was more determined than ever to get Mother and Dad to let me go.

"What plays are they doing?" I asked.

"I don't know yet. But whatever they do, I'll have a chance to audition. And I'll also get to do costumes and props and scenery and lights—and learn all about theater. And meet casting directors and agents. They all come, you know. They're always scouting for new talent."

"Then you won't get a job and earn money for college?"

"I don't need to. Summer stock is six hundred dollars but my parents don't mind paying for it because they believe in me. They think I have talent. And they'll pay all my college expenses, too. I'm going to go to a college that specializes in theater. What about your parents? How do they feel about your acting?"

"They think I'm terrific," I lied. I wondered if Helen could tell I was lying.

"Then I'll be seeing you there this summer. That's great! Stock would do you a world of good, Patty. If you had a season of stock under your belt before you tackled Juliet, you'd probably be doing a much better job. As it is . . . well, I suppose you're okay. After all, it's only a school play."

My mind was awhirl. Was I only doing an "okay" job with Juliet? Was my acting amateurish, high school acting? Ms. Howard said I was doing "a fine job." I felt very good about some of the scenes. Would I be any better if I'd gone to summer stock last year? Would Helen be better than I if she went this summer and I didn't? I was dying to talk to Mother and Dad again about summer theater and to convince them that I had to—I simply had to go.

"Helen's parents are paying the fee so she can go, and they're paying all her college expenses so she doesn't have to work."

"I don't care what Helen's parents are doing," Dad responded. "You're our daughter, and your mother and I make the decisions concerning you."

"But don't you understand? I need the experience. Kids like Helen will be getting a head start on me."

"A head start? Are you in a race?"

"Don't you understand? If I don't act in summer stock the kids who do will get all the good parts in next year's productions in school and I won't get any."

"You did pretty well for yourself with Juliet."

"I got the part but Helen says I'm not doing a very good job. That I'm 'okay for a high school production.' " I was nearly in tears.

"And since when is Helen such a judge of talent? She just sounds jealous."

I was relieved to hear Dad say that.

"You know," he continued, "whether you're a good

149

actress or not a good actress, one season of summer stock won't make a bit of difference. Your friend Helen probably imagines summer stock will make her a professional. It won't do anything of the kind. She'll probably spend her whole summer—and her parents' six hundred dollars—for the privilege of sewing costumes or running errands for their stars. Or maybe they'll let her clean the toilets."

"That's not what stock is like, Dad."

"How do you know? You've never done it."

"Neither have you."

There was a moment of silence. Then Mother spoke. Her voice was very soft as though she really didn't want to speak the words.

"You know, your Aunt Ruth apprenticed in a summer theater when she was just about your age. Our parents didn't want to let her go but Ruth begged them and pleaded and carried on till she got her way. That was the summer she got diabetes. We all traveled up to Maine to bring her home. Let me tell you, she was a very sick young lady. She nearly died up there. She was on the verge of a coma. They overworked her, she hardly got any sleep, the food was all starches and sweets—and she wasn't acting either. She had one walk-on part the whole summer. Mostly what she was doing was just what your father said: sewing costumes, painting scenery, running errands—and cleaning toilets. Believe me, it didn't make her a better actress. And it nearly killed her."

For a moment, no one spoke. Then Mother added, in a soft, half-choked voice, "It hurt all of us. Plenty. The whole family. After that nothing was ever the same." I wondered what she meant, but I was hesitant to ask. I thought she might start to cry. I understood how Mother felt, but it wasn't fair. She was preventing me from doing what I wanted because Auntie had gotten sick. It didn't make sense.

Dad must have read my mind, for he said, "Your aunt aside, Patty, we want you to earn some college money this summer. You've got to start learning to pay your own way. We're not going to support you forever."

I felt abandoned. "But Helen's parents are paying for her because they believe in her talent."

"I don't care what Helen's parents are doing. We're your parents."

"Don't you want me to succeed in life?"

"You will be succeeding if you're a responsible human being. A responsible adult who can support herself."

"Auntie never graduated from college and she supports herself."

"Your aunt was very fortunate. She's strikingly beautiful so she was able to get modeling jobs, which paid her well. To us, you're very beautiful, too, Patty. But I don't think anyone will pay you for it."

"And look at your aunt now," Mother chimed in. "How will she support herself now? She's got nothing to fall back on. No solid education, no degree. I don't know what she's going to do."

I had assumed she'd learn to walk again and maybe play old character ladies in wheelchairs or ladies who use canes or walkers. But now that I faced it, there weren't that many roles that called for disability. And then, they were probably played by able-bodied actresses pretending to be disabled or elderly. So what would Aunt Ruth do? But what would she do even if she had a college education? She wouldn't be happy doing anything but acting.

Mother and Dad exchanged glances. "We've been discussing this," Mother said, "and we're willing to help you pay for acting class if you'd like in the fall. You can pick out any after-school or weekend acting program—we'll let you go into the city for it. And for every dollar you pay, we'll match it. So don't think that we don't believe in you or that we don't want to encourage you. We want whatever will make you happy."

"Summer stock would make me happy," I mumbled, though I was genuinely surprised and grateful that they did offer help with my acting career. "Thanks." I smiled, in spite of myself.

I was anxious to discuss it with Aunt Ruth.

"It sounds terrific!" she said. "I'm thinking of taking acting class myself as soon as I'm back on my feet. Or maybe even before."

"Are you going back to the soaps and the modeling in Hollywood?" I ventured, not wanting to upset her with my question, but trying to understand her thoughts.

"Not exactly." She smiled. "I'm starting over. First on my agenda is learning to walk—perfectly. Without crutches. And as soon as I can, even in a wheelchair, I'm going to start taking classes and working on scenes. Hopefully, I'll be able to support myself with some modeling—above the waist, of course. Then, after we settle the divorce, I'm coming to live in New York."

How wonderful she was!

"I've had plenty of time to think about it." She sighed. "And you know what? I'll be so happy to be well and out of the hospital that I'll enjoy doing whatever I'm doing."

She amazed me! I couldn't picture myself happy anywhere but on the stage. It seemed like a self-betrayal. Like Mama's giving up music to get married.

"Could you have been happy before if you weren't acting? Is it different now or would it have been true before if you had to spend your life as a secretary or a waitress or something else?" I asked Ruth.

"I'd always be taking class, working on scenes, trying out for parts. But I think . . . in the meantime . . . I could find pleasure and happiness."

"In what? In going to an office every day and sitting at a desk?" I was getting angry. I was disappointed in Auntie. She was the one who always encouraged me. Was she now saying that all my dreams—and all of hers, too—didn't really matter? She was beginning to sound like Mother.

"What I mean is, I'll be happy just being able to walk and take care of myself. To watch the sun set or feel the rain against my skin—as a free woman, out of the hospital. I can enjoy all that, whatever else I may or may not be doing. One thing this hospitalization has taught me—to try to treasure every moment, to find something to enjoy, no matter how inconsequential, because life is so short. You know,

153

Patty, we only go around once. This isn't the dress rehearsal."

She has to feel like this now, I told myself. But I don't!

I didn't want to hear any more. I felt I was getting nothing but lectures from everyone—lectures on responsibility from Mother and Dad and a lecture on happiness from Aunt Ruth. Didn't anyone understand how I felt about acting? They were all trying to tell me it wasn't so important.

I must have sounded angry when I turned toward the door and said, "I better go now." For Aunt Ruth responded with, "Don't go yet, Hon. Stay awhile. I feel we left things . . . sort of . . . up in the air."

I wanted to stay, but I also wanted to give Auntie a hard time. "No we didn't. You said acting wasn't so important. And that I should be happy just because I can walk and I'm not in the hospital and that acting shouldn't be so important to me, either."

Auntie looked pained. I had succeeded in getting through to her.

"That's not what I said. That's not what I meant, anyway. Sit down a minute, will you? You're getting me nervous. I feel you're about to bolt out of here any second, as soon as you hear something—or think you hear something—you don't like."

This was the first time Auntie had scolded me. I wanted to cry.

"You mustn't be so quick to judge others," she remonstrated. "You want to be free to have your own feelings and your own aims and goals in life—then you have to accord others that privilege, too. I was

154

merely telling you how I see my own life—where I think I can find happiness. I wasn't—and I'm not—telling you what to do."

I kept quiet when she finished speaking because, although I understood what she was saying and knew she was right, I still felt I was being criticized and I didn't like it; I couldn't understand the sorrow she was rising above.

"Would you bring my wheelchair here please, Patty?" Auntie put on her robe and hip-walked to the edge of the bed, then pushed herself backward into the chair while I held it steady for her. She combed her hair and freshened her makeup and said, "Come with me. I want to show you something." She maneuvered the chair past the sink and the garbage can to the door and then out into the hall. I wondered what she wanted to show me. She wheeled herself down the hall and I walked beside her, past the nurses' station, the visitors' john, the broom closet and half a dozen patient rooms. We didn't stop until we came to the window at the far end of the corridor.

"I come here every day, a few times a day, and just gaze out the window and think. See those people down below? Sometimes I try to imagine where they're going and what their lives are like and sometimes I just think about my own life and all the changes in it. Those people rush right by and I wonder if any of them ever realize how fortunate they are to be outside the hospital, able to go where they want and do what they please. All I can think is how I'd love to be out there right this minute feeling the raindrops on my skin and sloshing in the puddles, maybe running for a bus—running, on my own two feet—maybe going to visit a friend or to take a class or go to the theater or just go home and make dinner and change into dry clothes and get comfortable. When you're confined in a hospital as long as I've been, even the simplest activities, like walking in the rain, take on . . . well . . . an aura of being wonderful—which they are, only ordinarily who bothers to notice or think about it? This is what I meant by finding happiness in everyday things. Sort of like Emily in *Our Town* when she returns to earth and suddenly she can see the beauty and the wonder in those everyday things she never noticed before."

Auntie turned and fixed her gaze on me. "So you see, Patty, I'm not telling you that your acting—or my acting—isn't important. I'm suggesting that it's not the only thing in life and that you should also try to derive pleasure from just being alive—from being able to walk and talk and breathe the fresh air and feel the rain and the snow against your cheeks." She paused a moment, and then continued very softly. I had to bend towards her a little in order to hear what she was saying. "I guess I feel as though . . . I'm coming back from the other side . . . like Emily. I came very close to dying. The gangrene could have traveled through my body and killed me. I feel as though I'm being given a second chance at life. And I want to change the way I relate to and appreciate life. I don't think I'll get a third go-round. So I want to make the most of this life."

We lingered by the window in silence long after Auntie stopped talking. I gazed down to the street below, to where two streets converged half a block from the hospital. One was a quiet, tree-lined street with private houses and a mailbox. A man was walking a dog. The other street was broad and heavily trafficked. A bus was waiting at the stop and another bus was turning in from a side street. I counted seven pedestrians, and they all seemed to be in a hurry. A woman and two little girls were half running as though they were being blown by the wind. I listened to the howling of the wind and the pelting of the drops against the windowpanes. Diamonds and pearls, I thought. And the two traffic lights in the street kept changing from emerald to gold to ruby red. I wondered if Auntie was seeing these things in the same way I was. Or was she lost in her own thoughts, contemplating her losses or the new life that lay before her? I wanted to ask her, but she seemed to have retreated into a private place and I didn't want to intrude.

After a while, my attention began to drift. I began thinking of other things—of my *Romeo and Juliet* rehearsals, of Roy, and of summer stock versus acting class. I grew tired of standing by the window. Auntie sensed my impatience; she reached for my hand and squeezed it.

"You ready to go back?" she asked softly.

"Uh-huh!"

She released the brakes, backed up and swung the chair around in the direction of her room.

I felt as though we were returning to Earth from a sojourn in some far-off place.

When I left Aunt Ruth, I decided to circle the block

157

and find the streets we'd been watching. I wanted to feel how it would be to actually enter into the scene I'd been observing, which seemed half real, half like a stage set, and what it would be like to become one of those characters who peopled the set and whom I'd tried to invest with a life of my own imagining. But the streets, when I found them, were not at all as they seemed from the window. I liked the window version better. Here, the rain did not glimmer as diamonds and pearls, but was merely cold and wet, and the traffic lights were not rubies, golds and emeralds. They were just traffic lights. And the exhaust fumes from the buses polluted the air. If only life could be the way it seemed, instead of the way it was! It would be so wonderful. I was excited by my discovery of a whole secret world—the world touched by imagination—that I had never known existed. I wanted to express it to share it with others—but how? Perhaps my excitement was like Juliet's when she discovered romantic love. But that was too general. I needed some concrete way to express my delight with the diamond and pearl raindrops, with the twinkling rubies and emeralds and with the inner life with which I'd endowed the mother with the two little girls. I wanted to share it all, yet keep it close in a very private part of me. I decided to try to capture it in a story or a poem; to write it.

18

I stayed up most of the night trying to find the right words, to re-create the magical aura of the raindrops. It was after four A.M. when I put down my pen, satisfied with what I had written. I switched off the lamp by my bedside and lay back on my pillow, trying to run the lines of my poem through my mind. But I fell asleep almost immediately.

All that week, I kept trying to put my feelings into words. I wrote one very short poem about love and started a story. And I began keeping a diary. There were things I needed to write about that I couldn't share in real life with anyone, not even Aunt Ruth. I found myself looking forward to those private times when I could write, even more than I looked forward to rehearsals and to working on my part. That alarmed me. I had always assumed I would be an actress. I would go to summer stock, attend scene-study class and I would rehearse with my fellow actors in plays where you could not deviate from the script and which, therefore, were safe. I had assumed

I would live for acting and the theater. But now I began questioning if that was what I really wanted. If I was not Patty the Actress, then who was I? I had no idea if my writing would mean anything to other people. Was I wasting my time? And even if it wasn't wasting time, did it mean anything? And what about Roy? I wanted our lives to be intertwined, but how could this happen if he was going to devote himself to the theater, where he would always be meeting beautiful young actresses—and I was off by myself writing? And if we weren't together most of the time, wouldn't he go back to Emma?

We were sitting in the auditorium watching the street-fighting scene between the Montagues and the Capulets when Emma came up to us. She was so beautiful it made me feel dwarfed.

"How are you doing, Roy?" she asked, ignoring me completely.

I could tell he was happy to see her.

"Pretty well, thank you, and you?"

"Looking forward to graduation. Aren't you?" She slipped into the seat on the other side of him. Roy turned to face her. I could have disappeared and he never would have missed me.

"Say, you got your hair cut or something, didn't you? It looks great!"

She giggled and shook her head, fluffing her hair. I looked the other way.

"When are you leaving for stock?" she asked.

"July Fourth weekend."

"Oh, good! So we have time to get together before then."

"Sure thing!"

"Take it easy now!" And she sauntered up the aisle to where she had been sitting.

I was nearly in tears but I didn't want Roy to see. I waited until I could control my voice before I spoke.

"Is she your girlfriend?" I asked, trying to sound casual.

"Not anymore. She used to be. But we're both graduating this year and we'll be going to different colleges. So we won't be able to see each other. She suggested that we start dating other people so we can each have a social life. But we're still good friends."

I felt my heart sink. I wanted to say, "Is that why you're bothering with me—to get in practice for the girls at school?" And I wanted to know how much he liked Emma and if he'd still be going with her if she hadn't wanted to split. But I didn't dare to ask him this.

He sighed. "I guess I do feel a little hurt—you know, rejected. But I'll get over that!" He grinned at me and touched my arm.

I still enjoyed rehearsing *Romeo and Juliet* but that was a very special play. The White Plains Stock Company had just released its summer schedule and they were all trite situation comedies. Nothing very interesting. I couldn't see myself spending all that time building scenery and working backstage and maybe getting to rehearse a few silly lines in a silly play. I'd much rather be using my evenings to write.

How much more satisfying it would be to actually write a book, to create characters and let them do anything I decided, than to act lines someone else had written. Who knows—I might write a book that people would read for generations to come! I might even write a play and go to see it performed on the stage. Certainly, writing could have a more lasting effect than acting, which is gone when the performance ends or when the play closes.

I didn't mention my change of heart to anyone. I could just imagine Dad saying, "I told you you'd never succeed as an actress!" Even though they had offered to help with my acting classes, I knew that wasn't what they wanted for me. And I was afraid Aunt Ruth would be disappointed in me. Although she encouraged me to enjoy other things in life besides acting, I knew she didn't mean for me to give it up. She wasn't giving up on acting despite her hardships. And I was afraid Roy might lose interest in me, since the main topic we talked about was theater.

Worse, I felt confused. I didn't really want to give up acting, but I felt torn between rehearsals and writing. Both seemed to occupy all my concentration, time and energy.

I was headed home after an early rehearsal one afternoon. We'd been reworking the scenes between Juliet, her mother, father and Nurse. I'd never realized how much comedy there was in Nurse's role. I'd assumed the entire play was an unending tragedy. Carmella, the girl playing the role, was perfect for the part. She was short and stocky and had a coarse quality to her voice. She kept half her teeth blacked out with licorice, which made her appear older and funnier, and she waddled when she walked.

Ms. Howard called her "a true character actress."

I was thinking about Carmella's acting and how we could all be equally talented, yet different, so I nearly bumped into Roy without seeing him outside the school.

"You look like you're in your own world," he commented.

"I was just thinking about rehearsals and how different we each are. How could Shakespeare dream up all these different characters? I'd love to be able to write like that!"

"Who wouldn't?" He laughed. "You and the rest of the world."

Then he changed the subject. "Where are you headed? I'll walk with you as far as the station if you're going that way. Then I have to detour to take a train to the city."

"Okay," I agreed enthusiastically, though I wasn't headed that way at all.

"I'm going to meet with the director of my summer stock company," he said. "The theater is all the way up in New Hampshire. He comes in once a year to meet with the company members and the apprentices so he can get an idea about casting."

"Are you doing an audition for him?"

"I don't think so. I think he just wants to meet with us and sort of get a feeling about what kinds of roles we can play. I don't know, maybe he'll ask us to read something. I always come prepared."

"Do you go to a lot of auditions?"

"No, not a lot, but a few, and I like to be prepared. I have two monologues and two very good scenes—

one comedy, one serious. But I need a partner for both of those scenes."

I wanted to say, "I'll be your partner," but I was afraid that might be too bold. Maybe he didn't want me as a partner; maybe he didn't think I was good enough. Maybe he preferred to work with Emma or perhaps the scene called for a man. Besides, if he wanted me, he would ask. And he didn't.

When we neared the railroad station, he left me. "See ya tomorrow!" he called. "Be good!"

"You, too!" I waved. Then I turned and headed home. I wished he weren't going to go away for the summer.

It was a week before I saw Aunt Ruth again. I could have made time to visit her during the week, but I was unsure how to tell her that acting was no longer my top priority, though I didn't really think she would disapprove.

I had decided to mention my writing casually, at the end of the visit, as I was leaving. Only I was beginning to feel a little unsure of myself, now that I no longer thought of myself as Patty the Actress. I wanted Auntie to read my poem and the half a story I had written and to give me her opinion. I considered telling her that someone else had written them or that I'd found them in a book, but Auntie was too smart for that.

She surprised me when I entered the room. She was sitting in a regular chair, her legs extended on boards and covered with a brightly crocheted mini-blanket.

164

Her copper hair, sparkling once again, softly crowned her head; ringlets dangled round her ears. She wore coral lipstick and tiny gold earrings. She looked more like the model and actress she was than like a patient, except for the pale, nearly translucent texture of her skin and the deep gray circles beneath her eyes.

But I was so eager to tell her about my writing that I didn't take time to comment on her appearance. Two minutes after I was in her room, I said, "I have something to show you!" and I removed the papers from my pocketbook and handed them to her.

She regarded me questioningly. "Is this for me to read now or later?"

"Now!"

I sat on the edge of my seat and scrutinized her face for a response. After she had read all three pages, she reread each one. It was all I could do to keep from crying out, "Do you like them or not? Please tell me, are they good?"

When she finished, Auntie looked at me as though she'd been reading my mind.

"They're lovely," she said. "Did you write them?"

"Yes. Do you really like them or are you just saying it?"

"I do. I really like them. I didn't know you could write. Have you written more?"

"Not really. I started writing after my last visit to you. Remember how we were watching the rain together? I kept thinking about that and how magical it was and when I got home I knew I had to write about it."

Aunt Ruth smiled.

"I'd like to see more of your writing," she said. "Show me that story when you've finished it."

"I will!"

"Did you show these to anyone else?"

"No. You're the only one."

"Well, you should. They're very good."

I wanted to show them to Roy but I was afraid he might laugh at me. I wasn't sure I knew him well enough. Even if he didn't laugh because he was too polite, he might not understand.

If I showed them to Mother, I was afraid she would just smile patiently and say, "It's lovely, dear. It's very nice." And then add, "Do you have any laundry to put in the load?" Or, "Do you want hamburgers for supper?" And Dad, he'd hand them back to me saying, "A lot of teenagers think they want to be writers. What makes you think you're any better than the rest of them?" He frequently said, "Whatever you do, you should be the best, or else not do it at all." And then he'd cite himself as an example. "If a patient comes to me needing heart surgery, I refer him to a heart surgeon. I could probably do it but that's not my specialty. A cardiac surgeon can do it better. But if he needs stomach surgery or an operation on his colon or his intestines or he needs his appendix removed, I do it because I feel no one could do it better."

"But Daddy," I argued, "it's not the same thing."

"The same thing as what? Sure it is."

"If it meant not acting or writing or painting or playing the piano unless you were the single best, then there'd only be one writer—probably Shakespeare—

166

and one painter, maybe Michelangelo or van Gogh."

At this point, Daddy would become very annoyed, shrug his shoulders and walk out of the room saying something like "If you want to settle for mediocrity in life, go ahead. I demand the best!"

"Do you have a school literary magazine?" Auntie interrupted my thoughts.

"What?"

"I said, 'Do you have a school magazine?' If you do, then you ought to submit your poem."

"I'd feel silly if it wasn't accepted."

"So what? You've got to try. And if they don't take it, submit it somewhere else. Where would I be if I never went out on an audition because I was afraid I wouldn't make it? Most of the time I don't get the part, but when I do, it makes it all worthwhile."

I knew Auntie was right when I thought about how happy I'd been to get the role of Juliet and how glad I wasn't so discouraged by not getting the lead in *Our Town* that I didn't try out for anything again. I decided to look at some back issues of *The Scarsale High Literary Journal* to see how my writing compared to other student writers'.

We were into the final weeks of rehearsal. They were all costume rehearsals now so we could get used to moving around in long dresses without tripping and so the boys could get used to wearing tights without feeling self-conscious. The closer we came to opening night, the more excited I grew—and the more nervous about my lines. What would I do if I forgot one of them? I couldn't possibly ad lib because the poetry

167

of the language was so important. I was afraid of making a fool of myself in front of everyone. I was so worried I spoke to Ms. Howard about it. I realized that if I were just writing and not acting before an audience, I wouldn't have to be so scared about making a mistake. I could always rewrite and take as much time as I needed. But in acting you can't do that. It has to be right the first time.

"You're doing very well," Ms. Howard assured me. "Just block everything else out of your mind while you're working. And listen to what the other characters are saying. I think you're doing that already. Listen to them and don't worry about your own lines. You know them very well. Think about what you're saying—but don't worry about it."

The next time I saw Roy, I confided in him. "I'm so nervous whenever I think about it, my hands turn to ice."

He grinned. "Are you nervous right now? Let's see." And he reached for my hand and took it in his. His skin was warm and amazingly soft and smooth for a boy's—as though he used lotion or something. He rubbed my hand gently between his palms. I felt myself flushing from head to toe.

"Warm enough?" he asked. My hand was very warm now, but his stroking was so sweet and soft, I didn't want him to stop.

He looked into my eyes and said, "Let me have your other hand now so it won't be jealous."

But just then, Emma appeared. She must have been watching us. She was slightly breathless as though she'd just dashed across the auditorium.

"Roy, can you come here with me a minute? I want to show you something."

"What is it?" he asked, still holding my hand.

"I can't tell you. It's very important. Just come back to my seat with me for one minute. It won't take long."

"All right. Excuse me, Patty." He gave my hand a squeeze as he stood to follow Emma. I looked up the aisle after them. Then I turned back towards the stage because I didn't want it to be obvious I was staring. But I couldn't help wondering what it was she wanted to show him and longed to know whether he preferred being with her.

"Act two!" Ms. Howard called. "Romeo, Mercutio, Benvolio—onstage, please! Juliet, in the wings!"

My long dress got caught in the seat as I stood and I nearly tripped. I felt like a klutz. What if it happened onstage during the performance? I gathered the folds in my hands to raise the skirt off the floor as I hurried to get onstage.

"Patty, I want you to practice moving in your costume," Ms. Howard said. "After rehearsal, take a few minutes to practice walking and getting up from a chair before you take off your costume. And that goes for all the girls! Be sure you feel comfortable in your costumes."

The boys were elegant in their tights and capes. It was easy to believe they were medieval young noblemen rather than twentieth-century high school juniors and seniors. I watched every move my Romeo made. He was so handsome in his tights! He was tall and lean, his legs were lithe and muscular like a dancer's and he moved so gracefully. I listened as the lines

169

floated into the wings. "Can I go forward when my heart is here?" If only he meant it, I thought. If only he'd give up his plans for going away this summer so he could be with me. But I half suspected that if he didn't go to stock and he remained in Scarsdale, he'd probably be with Emma.

The stage was bathed in pale blue moonlight. Nighttime. Juliet's orchard. I could almost smell the honeysuckle and the fruit trees. In my long gown and fancy headpiece, I could believe I had been dancing at a ball. I had met a handsome prince. I was in love.

Benvolio: Go then. For 'tis in vain
To seek him here that means not to
be found.

Exeunt: Benvolio and Mercutio.

Romeo: He jests at scars that never felt a
wound.—

My cue: Juliet appears above at a window.

Romeo: But, soft! What light through yonder window breaks?
It is the east, and Juliet is the
sun!—

I listened intently as Romeo poured out his longing. Oh, that it were true! As long as he remained Romeo, and I Juliet, there was no Emma to interfere.

19

The next afternoon as I was walking through the center of town to buy more makeup, Roy caught up with me.

"Hi, Juliet." He grinned.

"Hi, Roy. How are you?"

"Fine." Then he was silent as though searching for words. Finally, he said, "If I were you, I'd be careful around your friend Helen. She's going around telling everyone that the only reason you got the role of Juliet was because Ms. Howard felt sorry for you because she knew how much you wanted to play Emily in *Our Town*. I don't believe one word of that," Roy continued. "I think you're damn good and you were certainly better than any of the other girls who tried out, but I think you should be wary of Helen."

I was stunned. "You heard her say that or are those just rumors?"

"I didn't hear it personally, but two friends whom I trust told me because they know we're together a lot and they figured I could warn you."

I felt my face squeeze up into a knot as I began to cry. I didn't want Roy to see me this way.

But he understood. He held my head against his shoulder.

"I wouldn't waste too many tears over her, Patty. I think your friend is just a little jealous. A lot jealous, if you ask me. Every girl in the school wanted that part."

When I grew calm again I said, "Thanks, Roy, for telling me about Helen . . . I guess. I mean it wasn't really something I wanted to hear."

"Yeah, I know. But I thought I should warn you. Why don't you face her and ask her about it?"

"Nah. Not now, anyway. She'd probably just deny it."

"Maybe not. Try it and see."

But I was afraid she wouldn't deny it and that would mean the end of our friendship. I remembered what good, close friends we used to be and I didn't want it to end. As long as I didn't confront her, perhaps I could just ignore what she was saying and we could continue being friends. Maybe it was all just a bunch of rumors, anyway. I didn't feel comfortable with this decision but it was the best I could do for now.

"What do you say we change the subject with a couple of ice cream sodas?" Roy suggested.

"Fine with me!"

As we sat down at the counter of Sam's Sweet Shoppe, I couldn't help thinking of the drugstore scene in *Our Town*. Only we weren't Emily and George, and we didn't discuss our life plans or how much we cared about each other. Rather, we talked

172

about summer stock and school. When we finished our sodas, Roy walked me home. I wanted to invite him inside to continue our conversation, but I was afraid he might refuse. So I just said, " 'Bye. Thanks for the soda and everything. See you tomorrow."

" 'Bye. See ya!"

For the next few days, I avoided Helen and I noticed she avoided me, turning her head the other way when she caught sight of me. During rehearsals, I kept imagining she was watching me and pointing out to her friends what a poor job I was doing. After a while, I stopped enjoying rehearsals. But opening night was still three weeks off and there were lots of rehearsals coming up.

By the end of the week, I was feeling depressed— almost too tired to attend rehearsals. But I went anyway, and did the best I could.

Ms. Howard noticed the difference in my acting. "Aren't you feeling well?" she asked.

"I'm all right. I'm just tired."

"Maybe we're working you too hard. You ought to try to get more sleep. Take a nap when you're not rehearsing."

She seemed to forget I had homework and studying to do for my academic subjects.

Saturday I decided to stay away from the evening rehearsal. The thought of encountering Helen was too unpleasant. And besides, I would rather be writing something of my own than reciting lines someone else had written. So I phoned Ms. Howard and told her I wasn't feeling well and didn't think I could make rehearsal.

"Don't worry about it," she said. "Get yourself some sleep and then by Monday's rehearsal you'll be fresh as a daisy."

I felt bad about lying to Ms. Howard. But then, I told myself, I'm so tired that I really don't feel well.

I spent the whole morning trying to write a story, which I tore up three times because I didn't like the way it was coming out. Finally, I decided to give up on the story for a while and write in my diary instead. It always gave me a feeling of relief to commit my feelings to paper.

At the supper table Mother surprised me by asking how rehearsals were coming along.

"Pretty well," I replied. "Only three more weeks and we'll be ready to go." I wondered if I looked guilty at Mom's mere mention of rehearsals.

After dessert, I got up to leave, wishing them both a good night.

"Have a good one," Dad said. "Make me proud of you."

"I'm going upstairs to get something, then I'm leaving." I kissed them both on the cheek, then went to my room and closed the door. I knew in a few minutes they would think I had gone.

I sat down at my desk and tried to write but I couldn't concentrate because I was too busy worrying about rehearsal. Who was filling in for me tonight? I hoped it wasn't Helen. Whoever it was, I hoped she wasn't good. What if Ms. Howard decided she was better than me and she wanted to give her my part?

After a while, I lay down to think. Was I sure I

wanted to be an actress? Of course! Was Helen my only reason for avoiding rehearsal? Yes . . . and no. I needed time to write. With all those rehearsals, I never had time for myself—for thinking and writing. Do I want to write more than I want to act? Do I want to write enough to give up acting? No! I want to do both.

I don't know how long I was lying there trying to work things out. I was so deep in thought I didn't even hear Mother come into the room until she spoke.

"Patty! What are you doing home? I thought you left a long time ago. Don't you feel well?"

I thought of making something up, like a stomach-ache, but I didn't want to lie.

"I'm exhausted. I didn't feel like going tonight."

"But you've got an obligation to be there."

"It's okay. I phoned Ms. Howard and she excused me."

"That's not the point." Mother sat down beside me on the bed. "Patty, what's the matter? This isn't like you at all."

"I just didn't feel like going. I wanted to write."

"You could write some other time."

"With all the rehearsing—and homework—there's no other time to write. And it's very important to me. I think I want to be a writer."

"And what about your acting?"

"I never thought I'd hear you ask that. I thought you didn't approve of my acting."

"That's got nothing to do with what we're discussing. Didn't you realize that when you accepted the role of Juliet—or any role—you were accepting the obligation to attend rehearsals and stick with it? You can't boycott rehearsals whenever you feel like it. It's not fair to the others or to the production."

"I don't need a lecture about boycotting rehearsals. This is the only rehearsal I've missed."

Mother was silent. Then she replied softly. "I'm sorry. I didn't mean to lecture you. I was only concerned. Are you sure everything's all right?"

I was just about to say, "Sure, I'm sure," when I burst into tears.

Mother put her arms around me and drew me close. She didn't ask questions, but just kept comforting me with "Shhh, Shhh, Patty. Everything will be all right."

When I'd cried myself out and started to straighten myself, she pressed her cool cheek against my face, which was warm and wet with tears. I don't recall ever feeling so close to Mother.

I finally admitted, "I guess I stayed away because of Helen."

"Because of Helen? What's she got to do with it?"

Then I explained how Helen had been telling all the kids that I'm not a good actress and that I only got the part because Ms. Howard felt sorry for me.

"First of all," Mom said, "you are a good actress. The other students can see that for themselves. Second of all, why should you be concerned with what Helen says? She's jealous, that's all."

That was the first time I'd heard Mother defend my acting. It made me begin to feel better.

"Third," Mother continued, "or rather, it should be

first. Don't you know you can't just walk away from a relationship with no word of explanation? You've got to own up to your actions. You have a relationship with that play, with your fellow actors, with Ms. Howard, with Juliet. You can't just turn your back and walk away. You have a responsibility. Even to Helen. The responsibility of friendship."

"Then she has the responsibility of friendship to me, but she broke it."

"I don't care what Helen did. I care about you doing the right thing."

"So what's the right thing? You want me to apologize to her for her wrongdoing?"

"No. I want you to face her with what she's done. I don't want you running away from her."

"She'd only deny it."

"Maybe so. But maybe it's not true. Maybe someone started the rumor about her. Did you ever think of that? And even if she did say all those things, it's better to face her and ask her why."

"We could never be friends again after that."

"Do you consider her your friend now? Someone you trust?"

"No."

"Then what have you got to lose?"

I knew Mom was right, but I dreaded a confrontation with Helen. At least this way I could pretend we were still friends or that we would resume our friendship again someday. But once I confronted her and she got angry and maybe we'd argue—that would be the end of our friendship forever.

177

Long after Mom left the room, I lay on my pillows trying to decide what to do.

I would have liked to turn back the clock to the way our friendship used to be. Before Juliet. Before Emily. The way we were right now was nothing. Not friends. Not enemies. Maybe if we had it out, we'd clear the air. I doubted it. But at least I'd know I'd tried.

20

Monday afternoon, on the way home from rehearsal, I caught sight of Helen half a block ahead of me. I quickened my pace to catch up with her. She turned with surprise when she saw me. I tried to act casual, though I wasn't feeling the least bit casual.

"Hi, Helen."

"Oh, hi."

I didn't know how to continue. My mouth was dry and my elbows and knees were trembling slightly as I searched for words. Finally I asked, "Are you mad at me?"

"No. Why? I thought you were mad at me."

"No." This was the moment to tell her what was on my mind. "Not mad exactly. But, well, upset. I heard you've been telling everyone that I'm not a good actress and that the only reason I got the part of Juliet was that Ms. Howard felt sorry for me."

"I'm entitled to my own opinions, Patty. If I don't think you're a good actress, that's my right. And if other people agree with me, that's their right, too.

And I don't remember saying anything about Ms. Howard feeling sorry for you. You've got that all wrong."

"What did you say then?"

"I was explaining the meaning of repertory to the other kids. That you've got to give all the actors a chance to shine so that if an actor had a small part in one play, like you did in *Our Town,* the director is obliged to give that person a starring role in another production. That's all I said. I didn't say a word about Ms. Howard feeling sorry for you. Though she probably does."

"Why should she feel sorry for me?"

"Because she knows how much you want to be an actress and you're just not good enough."

I felt my throat begin to tighten and my eyes to water.

I couldn't reply. Maybe she was right. Maybe I really wasn't good enough. Yet I knew how deeply I felt the part of Juliet and I believed I had talent. This discussion with Helen wasn't helping me any. She was making me doubt myself when I knew I was good.

I didn't want to hear any more from her so I said, "I guess you're entitled to think any way you like, but I don't happen to agree with you. So maybe there's no point in this whole conversation."

"Wait a minute. I have a few things on my mind, too. How do you think I felt about your dropping me completely when you were cast as Juliet? I understand you didn't have as much time for me with rehearsals and all but you didn't have to ignore me completely. You just walked around with your nose

180

up in the air like no one was important enough for you—except Roy."

"That's not true. I wanted to be friends with you, but you were always with a new group of girls."

"So what? Were you jealous?"

"No. I just didn't think you wanted me around."

"That's ridiculous! If you wanted to be friends, you would have come over to us. But you were too busy being 'Ms. Juliet' and you were too good for us. You were too good for the whole world! Ask any of the kids. They'll all agree with me."

"I didn't mean to be a snob. I'm sorry it seemed that way to you." I didn't know whether to laugh or cry because the idea was so far from the truth.

"Well! Now that you apologized, we can be friends again," Helen declared. I didn't realize I had apologized, nor had I meant to. But I was happy that Helen still wanted to be my friend.

21

The whole business of Helen and her jealousy bothered me—as did the possibility of my own jealousy of her playing Emily in *Our Town* and of her popularity with the other kids. I decided to speak with Aunt Ruth about it.

She was watching the late afternoon soaps when I came into her room.

"Hi, Sweetheart." She reached out to hug me. "See what I'm watching? One of the soaps I used to work on. I just caught a glimpse of Johanna in an extra role as a juror. I guess I'm a little jealous."

I sighed. It was as though she was reading my mind. "That's just what I want to talk with you about," I said.

"What's that?"

And then I launched into the entire story about Helen and me. I concluded with, "I still don't know whether we're really friends or not."

"It's tough when jealousy comes between friends,"

she sympathized. "Show biz is like that. Acting, singing, directing, it's all the same. In any profession that's highly competitive, there's bound to be a lot of jealousy and a lot of gossip. So, what are you going to do about it?"

"I don't know," I said miserably.

"I don't mean you specifically. I mean, what are the choices?"

I shrugged. "I don't know. I hate to lose a friend because of my acting. But I'd hate to give up acting because of a 'friend.' I mean, I prefer writing anyway. I'd rather spend my time writing a story or a poem than rehearsing a play. But that's not the point."

"No, it isn't. Not only that, but it won't get you out of competition or away from jealousy. There will always be someone who wishes she had written your book instead of you. But, of course, that's ridiculous. She might write some other book that is better—or worse—but no one can write your book except you. And if she's jealous because she can't write as well as you, you should be flattered.

"Now then, when was the last time you felt jealous when someone else gave a beautiful performance or a better audition than you did?"

I didn't have to think long about that.

"So you and Helen have each had your turns being jealous of each other."

"Yes, I guess."

"For sure! So don't be too harsh on her. That doesn't mean you have to trust her and confide in her if she made up stories about you. But just remember the

183

pain your own jealousy caused you, and don't be too harsh on her. Remember, you chose a competitive profession."

I didn't want to hear that. I wanted Aunt Ruth to sympathize with me and tell me that Helen was jealous because I was a better actress than she was. I wanted Ruth to give me answers. Should I quit the play and devote myself to writing? Should I ignore Helen from now on? What should I do about acting as a career? All these issues were tumbling around in my head and I wanted answers right away. But they weren't forthcoming.

22

Three days before opening night, I stopped being able to sleep at night. I was too nervous and too excited. The morning of the performance I wanted to stay home and rest, but Dad insisted I go to school. "If you're not well enough to go to class, then you're not well enough to perform tonight," he said. I dragged myself out of bed and set off for school.

I telephoned Auntie three times between classes, just to hear her voice and try to calm myself. I'd been hoping that somehow she'd be able to attend the performance. Perhaps Mother and Dad could take her in the wheelchair. But the hospital wouldn't allow it.

When I got to the girls' dressing room that night, I found a single, long-stemmed red rose at my place. There was a note beneath it. "To Juliet, 'Break a Leg!' Romeo." I wanted to throw my arms around him, to feel him close and have him call me his darling Juliet.

I grew excited thinking about Roy thinking about me. I knew how Juliet felt. Giddy with love, almost lightheaded. Sensing that something momentous was about to occur. It was a combination of Roy and opening night.

I checked to make sure my costume was there in its place on the rack before I started taking off my regular clothes—the clothes of twentieth-century Patty. I had worn my favorite dress to the theater in the hope of going out after the performance with Roy.

It was peaceful backstage. But a sudden shrill peal of laughter erupted down the hall. It died down momentarily, and then from the boys' dressing room I recognized Roy's voice and his hearty laughter, and then came the high-pitched giggles again. A door slammed. And then Emma and three other actresses burst into the girls' dressing room. The clatter jarred my concentration.

Emma set a white rose down on the table by her place and went to look for a vase. I felt jealous. I was sure Roy had given her the flower. So I wasn't that special to him, after all. There were rumors backstage that a talent agent was coming to the performance and someone from the casting department of CBS. This could be my big chance! Suddenly, once again, I wanted acting more than anything. I could always write in my spare time. But I couldn't always act unless a casting director thought I was good enough to give me a role.

Hysteria mounted backstage. Everyone clattering at once. Lots of nervous speculation about the talent scouts. Two girls were missing parts of their costumes; one girl's makeup had disappeared. And everyone was angling for a view in the full-length mirror. Lady Capulet's zipper got stuck. Ms. Howard came in to help calm us down and solve some of the last-minute emergencies.

"Half an hour!" she announced. "Break a leg, everyone!" That was an expression I generally hated, except when Roy wrote it in the note. It's supposed to mean "Good luck! Have a good performance!" But I'm convinced it originated with an understudy wishing the star would "break a leg" and then trying to cover up the curse by explaining that it meant "Good luck."

"Five minutes! Five minutes, everyone! Places! Places!"

I took one last look at myself in the mirror. Satisfied that I really did look like Juliet, I left my place at the makeup table and walked to the door. I was still nervous about tripping over my dress and forgetting my lines. Roy was waiting for me on the way to the wings.

"Hi, Beautiful," he greeted me.

I blushed. "Thanks for the rose. And the note."

He bowed gallantly, one leg extended, the other bent as the courtiers in medieval days did. He certainly looked the part of Romeo. " 'Tis nothing, m'lady." And then he asked, "You nervous?"

"Very."

"Me too." We walked towards the wings. He was to wait stage left and I, stage right. When we reached my waiting area, just behind the sight line, he leaned over and kissed me between my forehead and my cheek. It was such a soft kiss and so fleeting. Then he was gone. But I could still feel the kiss. Later that night, when I was in bed, the kiss still lingered. And for many nights thereafter.

I carried the kiss with me onstage and all through the performance. It helped me feel the part more.

The performance went well. It took me a few minutes to get into it and stop feeling nervous, and then I enjoyed every second. The audience cheered at the end. We all took four group curtain calls; then the principals took two; then they all cleared the stage, leaving Romeo and me to take the final bows. We held hands, and when he squeezed mine, we bowed together. Then, before we left the stage, each in the direction from which we originally came, Ms. Howard came onstage from the wings and handed Roy a bouquet of white roses, which he then presented to me. They were from Aunt Ruth but they seemed as though they came from Roy. As we reached our respective sides of the proscenium, stage right and stage left, we were to turn toward each other and blow a kiss. The audience cheered very hard for this—and then we were backstage and, after a few seconds, the applause died down.

I'd expected Roy would catch up with me on the way to the dressing rooms, but he didn't. The girls' dressing room was a rush of talk and laughter, everyone hurrying to get out of costume and into their street clothes so they could go out and party.

"Where's Emma?" someone asked after about fifteen minutes.

I glanced over to her place at the makeup table; it was vacant.

"I saw her backstage with Roy," someone else said.

I had a sick feeling in the pit of my stomach, sort of like my heart had just sunk down there. I wanted to cry but I just continued rubbing cold cream on my face in order to wipe off the makeup and pretended that I didn't hear the conversation.

It seemed to me that they still shared secrets together. Since she had coaxed him away from me in rehearsal that day to "show him something." I never did find out what that "something" was.

The dressing room was emptying out now. Most of the girls had left and were on their ways to parties or pizza or late night dates. No one had invited me. I'd been saving this night for Roy.

A few seats away, Helen was combing her hair.

"Where are you going tonight?" she asked. Then, not giving me a chance to reply, she continued. "I'm going for hamburgers with a bunch of the kids and then we've all been invited to a champagne and cookies party at Emma's house. But we're not going there for a few hours because she and Roy want some time alone." She sighed. "It looks like they're back together again."

"Oh, yeah?" I said, feigning a complete lack of interest.

"I'm glad," she said. "I think they make a lovely couple, both so tall and good-looking." She glanced in my direction to see what effect her words were having; I could see her in the mirror. I refused to look in her direction. I just kept applying my street makeup as though I didn't even know she was talking to me. But I couldn't wait for her to be gone so that I could let myself cry.

I don't need friends like Helen, I told myself. But yet, I felt abandoned.

189

And what about Roy? I wondered if he'd just been using me to try to make Emma jealous, or if he was practicing how to charm the new girls at college; or perhaps being loving to me helped him get into his part as Romeo. Or maybe he really did care for me but liked Emma more.

"I'll be seeing you!" Helen said as she put on her jacket and left.

Then I was alone. It was completely quiet backstage. Not even an echo, as though both worlds—the medieval, romantic world we had worked so hard to create onstage, and the real one, of nervous hysteria, giggling and hushed whispers—had suddenly died.

I was almost finished dressing but I worked slowly, although I knew Mother and Dad were waiting for me out front. I was still hoping that one of the agents might make his way backstage to talk to me. Or that Roy might find a way to get away from Emma and come to find me. But none of this happened. So, after a few more minutes of waiting, I determined to "put on a happy face," as Mother would say, and go out there and join the world.

23

The second performance was disappointing after opening night. No more flowers or rumors of agents or cheering; just good, solid applause, which ended as soon as we all got offstage.

Before the performance, Roy gave me a light peck on the cheek, but it lacked the sweetness and the feeling of opening night. He devoted most of his attention to Emma, keeping his arm around her as they walked to their places. I looked the other way because I didn't want it to upset my performance.

By the second and final weekend, some of the cast were fooling around during performance and muttering jokes under their breath. Those with smaller parts and walk-ons no longer seemed to care about the play. Everything was slipping. On the final night, even Romeo gave way. During the balcony scene, he whispered, "How do you feel about a beer?" The remark was so out of place, it nearly threw me. Then I was nervous, never knowing when to expect another curve. It came in the morgue scene when Romeo discovers

Juliet apparently dead and then takes his own life. When he rested his head on me, prepared to die, he whispered, "How about you and me boogeying out of here, Babe?" It wasn't funny, except that I was supposed to be dead and he was dying; I wanted to giggle. It was all I could do to suck in my breath and hold it in order not to start shaking with laughter. I was relieved when the final curtain came down and I had managed to remain "dead" throughout the scene. I wondered if Roy were purposely trying to make a fool of me in front of all those people. But why? Unless Emma had put him up to it. They left the theater together each night. She drove him home. He scarcely noticed me at all anymore. The last two nights he even forgot his little peck on my cheek before the show. I thought of the oft-quoted lines from the poem:

> For of all sad words of tongue or pen,
> The saddest are these: "It might have
> been."

How true they were! I wondered if Aunt Ruth ever thought about them. I decided to tell her about my aborted romance the next time I saw her.

"I don't know that poem," she said. "But I've often had similar thoughts. But for me, that's just fantasizing, just dreaming. Because things were never that good between Bob and me. I tried to convince myself they were, that we had the ideal marriage, but it was far from the truth. Now I just try not to think about it. What's the use? It won't change anything."

"I guess not." I had to agree. "But it must be hard."

"Yes and no. Sometimes when I'm just relaxing or daydreaming, and not really thinking about anything—suddenly, there he is and I don't know how long he's been there but I'm in the middle of some long scene with him. Sometimes it's very tender—lovemaking—and sometimes it's an argument." She sighed and her eyes had a distant look. But then she turned her attention to me. "When I'm in control of my thoughts, I have other things to concern myself with. Like learning to walk and getting on with my life. And you have other things to think about, too, besides Roy. Don't waste your energy on him. He isn't worth it. There will be at least a dozen more Roys before you choose the right one."

I knew Auntie was probably right, but I still cared for Roy—even though I was angry as hell at him. I felt abandoned although we'd never actually dated.

"Have you finished that story or written any more poems?" Auntie changed the subject.

"No. I've been too involved with the play."

"Well, now that that's over, you've got to make the time. No matter how busy you are. If it's really important to you."

I had been meaning to write about Roy in my diary, but somehow, I never got to it. When I wasn't working on *Romeo and Juliet* or studying for finals, I spent my time daydreaming. I had all kinds of fantasies. My favorite was how I'd write my first book during the summer—a romance. It would be published and when Roy read it, he would realize it was me he'd loved all along. Then he'd be sorry he left me and he'd come back and hug me so close, we'd feel each other's hearts beating. And then we'd start kissing—deep soul kisses. He'd give up his plans for going away to college so he could be with me.

"A penny for your thoughts!" Auntie snapped her fingers and laughed to bring me back to reality. I said, "Oh, nothing."

"Would you like to come with me to my therapy now? It's time for my P.T."

I brought the wheelchair to her bedside and she backed into it and we were on our way.

"I have a surprise to show you," Auntie said. "But wait until we're there."

When we got to the gym, she told me to sit in the waiting area a few minutes until she called me. Then she wheeled herself inside. I sat on the bench and waited. Roy and I were in each other's arms again, only this time we were sitting on my bed. He leaned against me till I lost my balance and tipped over backwards so I was lying flat. Then he put one leg across my legs and climbed on top of me. I felt the pressure of his entire body against me. And all the while we were kissing.

I don't know how long I sat there daydreaming, but suddenly Ruth's therapist was standing in the doorway talking to me. "You look like you fell asleep there." She smiled. "Your aunt said you can come in now."

There—standing up between the parallel bars—was Auntie—on legs! Not on steel rods with wooden shoes. Auntie was wearing regular sneakers on her feet. She looked fine—as she did before the amputations.

194

"How do you like them?" She was grinning broadly.

"Great! They look so real!"

"To me they look more like tree stumps painted pink. But they are legs—and they'll enable me to walk."

"These are only temporary prostheses," the therapist explained. "The permanent ones will be more cosmetic."

"Thank goodness for that! These are more like piano legs. They bulge in all the wrong places where no human leg bulges. I want my permanents to be nice and sexy."

"Tell that to the prosthetist."

"I certainly shall!"

"Let's get to work now. I want you to put all your weight on your right leg."

Auntie's face twisted in pain as she followed the therapist's instructions.

"Good! How does that feel?"

"Terrible! It hurts. The prostheses are too tight. They're killing me!"

"You'll get used to it. They're supposed to be tight. Otherwise they won't stay on your legs."

"But—I can't tolerate it!" She was sweating and her arms were trembling. She was beginning to stoop.

"Stand straight!"

"I can't! They hurt."

"Try!"

"All right." She straightened her back a little and then began bending over again.

"You've got to stand upright when you walk. You can't bend over like that. You'll fall flat on your face.

Now straighten your back and keep it straight.

"Good! That's much better." She called to two of the other therapists. "I want her to take some steps today. She may need a little extra support."

Tom got in front of Ruth and Myrna stood by her side ready to support her if necessary.

"Now, shift your weight to the left side and hold it," Wanda instructed.

"Good! Now back to the right. Okay. Now I want you to give a little kick with your left foot before you come down on it. Good—terrific! Now do the same thing with the right, like you're kicking a tin can— only don't bring your leg back. Keep it out there and step on it. Atta girl! Now do it with the left—terrific! Hey, you've just taken two steps!" Everyone applauded. I wanted to run to Auntie and throw my arms around her but I didn't want to disturb her concentration.

"Kick with your right again. Leave it out front. Step on it. Good. Kick left. Out front. Step. Wonderful!"

Auntie was shaking. "Please!" she begged. "Let me sit! They hurt—and I'm so tired. They're digging into my flesh. Please!"

"All right. You've done enough for today. You've taken four steps. Tomorrow you'll double it. But you may sit now."

Tom brought a chair and slipped it behind her and she slowly lowered herself into it. After a moment, the tension lines in her forehead and at the corners of her mouth relaxed—and she broke into a grin. "I did it! I did it!" she cried.

"You sure did!" Wanda agreed. "Why don't you skip

O.T. this morning? I'll tell Angie. Just go back to your room and rest. You worked hard."

"When do you think I'll be able to walk outside those bars? When will I be using a walker?" Auntie asked as they began removing her prostheses.

"First you have to walk longer distances inside the bars. Let's see your stumps." She examined Auntie's legs carefully. "Very good. But I think the prostheses are a little loose. Tomorrow we'll add more socks."

"Loose? They're too tight!"

"I told you, they have to be tight. Otherwise your stumps will keep rubbing every time you take a step. You'll get blisters."

Auntie groaned. "All right."

"You'll get used to it. I promise."

I wheeled Auntie out of the gym to the elevators. She was very quiet the whole way back to the room. Her shoulders sagged, she slumped in her seat. But I could tell she wasn't sleeping.

As soon as we got into her room, she broke down, sobbing. I'd expected she'd be exultant having taken her first steps. I put my hand on her shoulder. "Auntie, what is it? What's the matter?" But she went on crying as though she hadn't heard me, as though she didn't even know I was there. She sobbed as though her heart would break. "I want my own legs! I want them back!" And then, as though answering herself, "But I can't have them. They're gone—forever!

"No! I want them! I want them back—give me my legs! Please!"

I wondered whom she was begging.

"Please! I can't stand living like this! Why did you

197

take them away? Why? Please—give them back to me!"

Was she talking to herself? To God?

"My legs—my darling legs! You were so beautiful! I need you—I need you! But you're gone. I can't go on like this. It's too hard! Help me!"

She continued sobbing uncontrollably for a long while until exhaustion finally took over and reduced her to a whimper. And then to silence.

I considered tiptoeing out of the room. She didn't seem to know I was there anyway and I didn't want to embarrass her by letting her know I'd witnessed her breakdown.

But after a moment, she raised her eyes to look at me. "I'm sorry," she whispered. "I didn't mean for you to see me like that. Only I can't help it sometimes."

I bent down and kissed her forehead and gave her a hug. "Don't worry about it. I know it's terrible for you."

"Patty, Baby. I'm so scared. Everyone thinks I'm so brave but I'm really not. They admire how I keep on plugging away. But what choice do I have? I want a decent, normal, good life. Only sometimes—it's so hard! It seems impossible."

"But you're doing it."

"I don't know how much longer I can. Everything is such an effort. I can't even wake up in the morning and get out of bed like a normal person. If I want to get out of bed, I have to hip-walk to a chair. And it's agony to try to fit into those prostheses. I hate them! They don't even look like legs—and they hurt. How

198

will I ever be able to walk in them? It's so exhaust-
ing—I don't have the strength!"

I wanted to say something to comfort her but there
was nothing I could say. I was sure I wouldn't have
the strength, either. Her situation required superhu-
man will and courage. I wondered if anyone could
endure this, much less triumph over it.

24

I didn't see Auntie again until the day after my last final. Some of the kids had already split for the summer. The seniors were graduated. Roy was no longer around. Neither was Emma. I knew he was still in Scarsdale but I never ran into him. I missed him. I missed seeing him in the hallways during class change and the pleasurable excitement I would feel when leaving English, knowing we'd pass each other on my way to History and that he would smile or wave or tap me on the shoulder or the arm. "Hi, Juliet!" He persisted in calling me Juliet in the days after the play closed. I didn't mind. I liked it. Only now, it seemed centuries ago—like it happened in a different lifetime. School was all but ended for summer vacation. There were a few half days for returning books, getting report cards, cleaning out lockers and the like.

Aunt Ruth was at the parallel bars when I next saw her. She was standing independently, grasping both bars tightly. When she saw me, she smiled. She didn't dare lift a hand to wave.

"You came just in time!" she called "I'm about to do my mini-marathon. I'm going to walk the length of the bars and back."

The therapists walked alongside her in case she should need assistance, but she didn't. There was a chair waiting at the far end, and when she reached it, she carefully lowered herself into it. She slumped forward, and only then did I realize the effort her walk had cost her. After a moment, she reached for the bars and pulled herself up. Each step was pain; I could tell from the furrows between her brows and her tightly drawn lips. I came over to kiss her when she sat down. The therapists clapped and cheered her.

"This is the first time I walked so far," she told me. "I think they'll be discharging me soon for the rehab program. I don't need a hospital anymore. I'm not sick."

"What will you do in a rehab unit that you can't do at home?" I was disappointed that her homecoming would be postponed.

"I'll be learning all the skills I need to function in the world. Walking isn't enough. I need to be able to step on and off a curb, to climb stairs, to walk up and down hills, to reach for things without losing my balance, to sit and to stand up easily, to put on my own prostheses—oh, a hundred things! The world is a very complicated place."

Walking hills, climbing steps, getting on and off a curb—these things all came so naturally to me that I never gave them a thought.

Monday was the first day of my summer job. Mother had gotten me a typist-secretarial position in her office. We were driving to work together. My mind kept jumping from Aunt Ruth to me and back to Auntie and then to Mother. Twenty years from now, would I be much like either of them? If I had to deal with any of their problems, how would I manage? I thought of how happy Auntie was to be able to walk such a short distance. But not so long ago she used to run the Los Angeles Marathon, and I knew she used to go out running at least three times a week.

"What are you thinking about? You're so quiet this morning." Mother interrupted my musings.

"Aunt Ruth. She seems pretty happy. I was wondering how she does it."

"My sister does not believe in looking back into the past. She just goes her merry way."

Mother's reply didn't answer my question at all. Well, it did and it didn't. It veered off in another direction. I always wished I had a sister or a brother; a sister, particularly. We would be best friends, confide everything in each other, our deepest, darkest secrets. And we would try to help and encourage one another. If I had written a story or a poem, she'd read it and understand what I was trying to say. If I were in a play, she'd come to see it and cheer. If she were to get married, I'd be her maid of honor. And if she had children, I would be the kind of Auntie that Ruth was to me. And if ever we had misunderstandings, we'd settle them right away. I couldn't picture us carrying grudges for years on end.

Traffic was crawling when we reached the East River Drive. That gave me plenty of time to think.

202

Mother liked to be in the office by eight thirty. It was obvious she wasn't going to make it today.

We pulled into the garage at five minutes after nine. "There's no time to stop for anything. You can wait till the coffee cart comes around, can't you?"

"Sure." But I was already hungry.

Mother was a nervous wreck by the time we got upstairs, although a lot of the brokers weren't in yet. But she always liked to get her leftover paperwork done before nine thirty when the market opened and clients started to phone her. Mother had her own private glass-enclosed office on the northwest side of the floor. Her windowsill was lined with plants, which made it look like a greenhouse.

The summer progressed. I worked for three brokers, all men, on the southeast side. We got the morning sun. My first chore when I came in was to put up a fresh pot of coffee so it would be ready when the brokers came in and they wouldn't have to wait for the cart to come around. Then I'd water the plants that needed it and check to see if any of the men had anything urgent to go out. And then I'd take their mugs and bring them each their coffee.

My desk was situated in the outer office, just between their private offices, and as they needed me to type something or to fill out a form or do a mailing, they'd drop the work on my desk. "As soon as possible," one would say. Or, "Any time before four P.M. will do." Photocopying, addressing envelopes, stuffing them—day in day out. It was a boring job, but I kept at it all summer.

*   *   *

I hadn't seen Auntie in several weeks; the nine-to-five job didn't allow it. By the time we drove home and ate dinner, it was too late to set out for the hospital; visiting hours ended at eight. On weekends, when Mother went with Dad, I usually slept late, then spent most of my time writing and taking walks. I thought a lot during these solitary strolls; I thought about my life and what I wanted; I thought about college and acting class; about Roy and the men I might meet in college. And I thought about my writing. Sometimes I invented visits with Aunt Ruth and thought about the things I'd tell her and what she would say to me.

Auntie was doing her laundry when I arrived at the rehab unit. It was the first time in ages that I had seen her in regular clothes—a skirt and blouse instead of a shapeless hospital gown. She was seated in a wheelchair, a plastic bag of soiled clothes in her lap together with a box of soap powder. The laundry room was tiny; there was scarcely room for the two of us. She looked up and smiled happily at me as I opened the door.

"Patty, Sweetheart! I'm glad you came!"

"So am I. You look great."

"So do you, Baby. I know it sounds silly because you've only been working a short time, but you look like a young woman on her own. I'm proud of you."

"Have you started walking yet?"

"Oh, yes! I'm in the wheelchair now because I needed to carry my laundry and the detergent. But most of the time I use the walker. And in therapy, I'm practicing with crutches. As soon as I get my laundry started, we can take a walk, if you'd like."

"Sure."

"You know, it sounds silly, but I actually enjoy doing my laundry. Being able to do it for myself— and not having to wait for someone to help me— makes me feel very independent. I'm beginning to reenter the mainstream of life."

"It doesn't sound silly to me."

"Good. I never enjoyed doing the laundry when I had my legs. I hated it. But now it's become a real source of satisfaction. Even an adventure."

I smiled at her saying the laundry was an adventure. She was great!

We walked completely around the corridor, and then Auntie began to look pale and her steps became unsteady.

"Do you want to sit? I'll go get a chair."

"No, no. Thanks. It's all right. I want to try to make it twice around the corridor. That's the best way to build up stamina."

Her breathing was coming hard and she had to pause for a moment to rest. Finally, she said, "You win. Please get me a chair."

"Will you be all right if I leave you?"

"Yes, yes. I'll just hold on to the nurses' desk here."

I went to her room and brought back the wheel-chair.

"Good thinking!" she said as she sank into the seat. "Now I can stay seated while you do the work."

"Where shall I wheel you?"

"How about my room? We can relax there and talk. I haven't seen you in so long I want to hear all about the things you're doing. You're still writing?"

"Yes. When I have time."

"You have to make the time. How's the job?"

"It's okay, I guess. It's boring."

We talked all morning, until it was time for Auntie to go to lunch. Visitors were not permitted in the dining room during mealtime. I peeked in through the windows. It was a cheery, sunny room. The long yellow formica tables and the decorations on the bulletin boards added to its bright appearance. But there was something wrong, something missing. I couldn't decide what it was. Then I noticed—there were no chairs by any of the tables. Not a single chair in the whole dining room. I soon understood as I watched the patients wheel themselves to their places in their wheelchairs. Some, like Auntie, who were able to use a walker or crutches, waited by their places for the attendant to bring a chair.

When Auntie comes to our house, she won't have to stand and wait, I thought. And she'll be coming home soon.

25

At dinner that night, I got a phone call. "Patty? It's Helen! How *are* you? I began to worry because I hadn't seen you all summer. I thought surely you would come to see at least one of our productions."

"I was busy."

"Busy? With what? Your job is only nine to five, isn't it?"

"I had other things to do," I said. But it was only partly true. I did some writing evenings, but I stayed away from the White Plains Summer Stock Company because I didn't want to see Emma and the other kids from school. I knew I'd feel bad sitting in the audience while they were performing onstage.

"I'm giving you the opportunity to make up for it now," she continued. "We're doing an end-of-summer apprentice production—and guess who's got the lead! It's this terrific play that no one's ever heard of about a girl's school in Switzerland during World War Two. In the first act I play an orphan whom nobody likes. In the second act I'm a Gestapo officer. And in the third act I'm one of the teachers. They had to switch around like that to give everybody a chance. But I'm the only one with three roles! The producers invited all the top New York agents—so maybe I'll be on Broadway this time next year. Now tell me, how was your summer? You like office work?"

"It was all right. I earned a lot of money."

"Patty! I never thought I'd see you choose money over theater! You sure have changed!"

I didn't bother responding. I thought, Wait till she sees my first novel in print!

But I agreed to attend the play anyway. I didn't want her to think I was a sore loser or anything like that.

Auntie was discharged from the rehab unit the Friday before school started. Mother took the day off from work and we both went to pick her up.

"I'll go park the car. You start helping Ruth load her things into a wheelchair," Mother directed. "Try to work fast. I don't want to get a parking ticket."

When I got to her room, Auntie was sitting on her bed, weeping softly. I had expected to see her joyous at finally reentering the "real" world. She forced a smile when our eyes met.

"I am happy," she said. "I really am. But I'm also sad. I hate good-byes. And I'm scared, too. It's scary to go where there's no one to take care of me and I'll have to do for myself."

"We'll help you."

She held out her arms to hug me. I felt her still weeping against my chest.

An elderly patient, somewhat stooped and very despondent, shuffled into view. When our glances met, he backed away from the door.

After a while, Auntie drew in a deep breath and sighed. "I'm sorry for carrying on like this. But it's more than just summer-camp-type good-byes, know what I mean? The kind of friendships you form here, in this kind of place where you all have these hardships and obstacles to overcome, well, it's different—more binding—than other kinds of friendships. I mean, every time I made real effort to walk or to do stairs or even one single step, it was like I was doing it for everyone. Know what I mean? I felt I had to do it to show the others that they could get better, too. And now, I hate to leave them. I want to see them improve and reenter life." She dropped her voice. "And then there are those special friends you make . . . and even though you mean to keep up with them, you don't know if you'll really be able to. You each go your separate ways . . ." she trailed off, ". . . and never the twain shall meet . . . perhaps."

Mother bustled into the room. She wore that strained smile I recognized as her "tension face." "Haven't you gotten started yet?" she asked. "We only have fifty minutes on the meter and I'm parked three blocks away."

I was enjoying the mellowness of the moment with Auntie, and Mother crashed right in and disrupted it. She scolded us both as though we were irresponsible children. I felt myself stiffen.

Auntie dried her eyes hastily and said, "I'm sorry, Rachel. Let's get started." Mother and I loaded the wheelchair with the giant-sized plastic and brown paper bags, which were lined up, crammed to over-flowing, against the wall. I couldn't imagine how Auntie had accumulated such a multitude of posses-sions in just a few months. Besides clothing and toil-etries, there were a mound of books and magazines, art supplies, cards, plants, nature posters, two apples, a shabby stuffed teddy bear, a little girl doll in a blue and white checked dress, four notebooks and the blue slippers I had given her—in another lifetime, it seemed. I wondered why she still kept them.

"Where will you keep all that stuff once we get back to the house? We have no storage space, you know. You'll have to fit it all into the tiny guest room," Mother said.

"I know."

"Why don't you leave some of it here? A lot of it looks like junk, anyway. What do you need it for?"

Auntie looked stricken. "I need it!"

"Do you mind telling me why? It just makes a lot of work for everyone. Tell me why you need a stuffed teddy bear or what you plan to do with those slip-pers."

"I need them—please!"

Mother had already reached into one of the bags to remove the bear. Auntie cried out, "O, reason not the need!" I knew she was quoting from Shakespeare, but the pain was her own.

Mother sighed, but she let the teddy bear be.

"I'll go bring the car around to the front entrance. Patty, come with me. Bring the wheelchair. You can stand guard over the things until I've loaded them into the car. Then I'll sit double-parked while you help Ruth down in the wheelchair. You can pile the rest of her things in her lap. But we have to work fast."

"See you soon, Auntie," I said as I struggled to push the overladen chair down the corridor. Mother dashed on ahead to hold the elevator. As I rounded the corner, I nearly knocked down the forlorn gentleman I'd noticed outside Auntie's room a while ago.

I was downstairs with the baggage for about ten minutes, and when I came back to Auntie's room I was stopped short by the sight of the sad little man sitting beside Auntie on her bed, holding one of her hands in his and stroking it tenderly. Then he lifted it to his lips and kissed each finger, looking into her eyes when he had finished. She smiled and leaned in towards him and I knew she was telling him it was all right to go further. He put his arms around her and she pulled him close and they kissed one long kiss for at least a minute. I didn't think old people could kiss like that. Then he jumped up and scurried to the doorway. I backed off in the nick of time to make it appear as though I had just arrived.

Auntie was fluffing her hair when I entered. She looked up and smiled. But she didn't say a word about her gentleman caller. I wondered if this was whom she meant when she spoke of "special friends" and "You each go your separate ways and never the twain shall meet." Was he the reason for her tears a little while ago? I couldn't understand her attraction to him though I could certainly see what he admired in her. But Auntie kept silent.

During the two months she stayed with us after the

rehab unit, she would occasionally go off alone in a taxi once she was getting around independently. She never said where she was going on these occasions. She usually stayed away a few hours and she was always very quiet and dreamy the remainder of the evening when she returned. I was sure she was going to visit HIM. But she never shared her secret.

26

Saturday night we had reservations for the White Plains Summer Stock Company. Aunt Ruth couldn't do stairs yet so Dad carried her down to the garage like a sack of potatoes over one shoulder.

Going anywhere with Auntie was an adventure in ingenuity because she couldn't do anything in the accustomed way.

I slipped into the backseat easily, swinging my legs inside and tucking them under me. Auntie could neither swing nor tuck. She turned with her backside toward the car door and shakily relinquished one crutch to Mother before feeling with her hand for the seat beneath her. She lowered herself cautiously and, once she was sitting, attempted to drag her prostheses inside. But she hadn't sufficient strength in her upper legs and the prostheses were clumsy and seemed to resist her efforts. Finally, she had to reach down with her hands, grasp each artificial limb around the calf and pull herself into the car.

I thought of how embarrassed I would be in her

place if anyone were watching me. But she didn't seem to be thinking of that. She heaved a sigh of relief once she was settled. "I'm ready!" Mother slid into the front seat beside Dad and we started.

Dad dropped us off in front of the theater so Auntie wouldn't have far to walk. But getting her out of the car was another hassle. Her legs had somehow gotten wedged in behind the back of the front seat. She struggled to extricate them and then to turn to face the door and set them before her on the sidewalk. She pushed herself up from the seat while Mother pulled her forward by one shoulder and arm. She had to rest leaning on her crutches to catch her breath before she could take even a single step.

"I guess I've gotten my exercise for the day!" she joked. But we still had to walk around the corner to the special "Handicapped Entrance," which was a steep ramp rather than the four stone steps of the main entrance. We waited for Dad to park the car so he could help with the hill. He followed behind ready to catch or to support Ruth, while Mother and I each walked to one side of her. When we reached the entrance, she needed to rest again. Once inside, we found ourselves at the rear of the auditorium. Our seats were third row center. It was another long, steep aisle to the front of the theater. Auntie groaned softly as she surveyed the distance.

"You can do it!" Dad encouraged.

"Going downhill makes me feel like I'm going to fall flat on my face."

"You won't. I'll walk in front and catch you if you start falling."

214

She had to walk sideways down the aisle in order to keep her balance, but we finally reached our seats. I sat between her and Mother, and as the houselights started to dim I noticed her shoulders sag and her eyelids droop. But then she stirred herself and sat forward eagerly in her seat. During the course of the performance, I think I watched Auntie as much as I did the actors. At one point, she closed her eyes and it almost seemed as though she were asleep. But her head remained erect and so I knew she was just withdrawing into her own thoughts. I wondered if she was wishing herself back in the Rehab unit where life was relatively easy; was she contemplating the rough road to recovery that still lay ahead of her; was she planning her future, her "handicapped," husbandless future, or was she thinking about the lonely old man who loved her, and was she missing him now? Or perhaps she was contemplating the steep climb up the aisle that awaited her when the play ended, and she was wondering whether the evening was worth the effort. I was occupied by my own thoughts of school and the beginning of my senior year, of the acting class I wanted to take, the stories I wanted to write, the boys I might meet, college applications. I could scarcely concentrate on the drama onstage; my own personal one seemed so much more important and more real.

When the curtain came down on act 1, Auntie reached for my hand and squeezed it. We remained holding hands, waiting in silent anticipation for act 2 to begin.